# ENSLAVELD
# BRAINS

## ALSO BY EANDO BINDER

*Adam Link, Robot*
*The Double Man*
*The Eando Binder MEGAPACK®*
*Enslaved Brains*
*The Forgotten Colony*
*The Impossible World*
*The Mind from Outer Space*

### THE SAUCER SERIES

*Menace of the Saucers*
*Night of the Saucers*

# ENSLAVELD BRAINS

## EANDO BINDER

**WILDSIDE PRESS**

# CHAPTER I

From the top of a tumbled rock ridge, Earl Hackworth pointed down into a long, barren valley.

"There's my ship," he said. "Isn't it a wonderful sight in primeval country? Like a jewel in a setting of lead."

His blue-eyed companion studied the object which indeed glinted like a fiery gem in the strong sunlight, but he made no answer.

Far back was the green spreading jungle—the cruel, hot jungle which it had taken them three agonizing weeks to traverse. It seemed to crouch like a savage beast, relentless, waiting. It hurled defiance to man, but man had won. From its edge to where the two men stood was sickly scrubland, accursed by nature, avoided by even the lowly snake. It had been as hot as the inside of a furnace and deceptively long. It had seemed to mock their dragging limbs and vanishing water supply. Even the jungle was better.

But that was all over now. Jungle and waste had been conquered; danger and suffering had buffeted them and left them weaker in body but stronger in spirit. Before them was but a short trip to the valley of naked sand. Then a man-made thing, an incredible marvel in aboriginal Africa, would take them up and away from feverish lowland jungle, from heartless scrub wastes, leaving them only a bitter memory.

"Well, Williams," Hackworth said to the blue-eyed man, "how do you like my ship?"

"Your ship!" Williams repeated, his eyes unfocused from his inward concentration.

"Yes, the ship I told you about," Hackworth said. "The ship that will take you from exile. It's a Sansrun, or helicopter airplane, and can rise vertically—vastly different from the planes you'll soon remember from years ago, Williams, that had to have a runway for taking off. Do you understand, old boy, or am I still talking too fast for you?"

"I can—understand," Williams said, his words slow and precise.

"Good," Hackworth said. "In another few weeks you won't have any trouble at all. Forty years is a long time... Now let's get the boys and finish our trek. You call 'em, Williams. You speak Bantu better than I ever hope to. Just two more hours, and then—farewell to Africa, jungle, and sand."

But Williams made no immediate move to call the "boys," or native *safari* men. Some strong emotion had gripped him. On his tanned face, darkened to a coffee color, was an odd expression of dismay, almost of fear.

"What's the matter?" Hackworth asked sharply. Williams muttered something in native dialect as his blue eyes glazed with his strong feelings.

"Listen here!" cried Hackworth. "Out with it. Something's bothering you."

Williams turned an agonized face to him. "I can't do it!" His voice was high and jerky; his throat muscles worked spasmodically. "Africa, Olgor... it belongs to me... I belong to it! *Musri et kraal*! How can I leave my home?"

Hackworth was thunderstruck. He stared at the brawny Williams and saw handsome features tightened with inner pain. Could this man have once been the eager, joyous cousin of his boyhood?

Hackworth stretched forth both hands, grasping the man by the shoulders.

"You *don't* belong here!" he said firmly. "You are my cousin. You were born far from this continent of mystery and misery. You are an exile here, and your natural heritage calls you!"

"I'm afraid!" cried Williams suddenly. "Forty years... I'm afraid to go back!"

Hackworth shook him, none too gently. "Afraid? Of what?"

Williams gulped. "Civilization... I wouldn't fit... I'm only an American by birth. At heart, after forty years, I'm like our *safari* boys—like M'bopo."

"Dan!" The name was wrung out of Hackworth by his cousin's outburst. Yet that name had power; it rolled the mists away from Williams' memories.

"Dan!" Hackworth repeated eagerly, seeing that he had fanned a spark. "Dan, you remember? Kids in Baltimore—how we played together, fought together? We were pals... Dan, how can you say you belong in Africa?"

The blue eyes glistened, looking back upon a life that had been buried under a landslide of later impressions. Williams smiled weakly. "Of course you're right. I'll go start the boys off."

As Williams left with a firm step, Hackworth was thinking that not until that moment had either of them realized what they were to each other. "Hackworth" and "Williams" they had called each other as strangers. Forty years of Africa had set up a barrier; only that name "Dan" had pierced the wall of time.

Williams got the *safari* men started with their heavy packs, down the winding trail of crumbling sandstone. The two Americans brought up the rear with rifles. A new eagerness was in all of them, tired though they were from the three-week trek from the heart of the Congo. The spearing glint of the airship in the valley promised rest and ease. They would reach it before sundown. Back of them the upflung ridge of wind-worn rock blotted out the jungle.

Forty years before, Dan Williams, eighteen, had left the United States with his father, on an exploration into the Congo. His father had had two purposes in mind—to penetrate the jungles just above the northern bend of the Congo River, and to find some trace of a previous expedition which had gone in there and never returned.

They came upon Pierre D'Lawoef, sole survivor of the other expedition, with friendly Bantu natives, but he was dying from knife wounds. A wandering tribe of Zulus had destroyed his five companions and their native boys. He had managed to escape and had lived with unwarlike tribes for eight years. But just before the Williams' expedition had come, the Zulus had reappeared and given the Frenchman his death wounds.

The elder Williams began to fear for the safety of his own party and gave the order to trek back to the river. But too late, for screaming Zulus with hideous painted faces had puffed out of the jungle and attacked with kris and spear. Rifle fire drove them off only after three of the expedition and a dozen *safari* boys had been killed, outright, and the others wounded.

Dan Williams had seen all this, and not long after had seen his father die of infection, leaving him the sole survivor of the expedition. Kindly Bantu natives adopted the orphan white boy, and forty years of Africa had made him a native in all but birth. He became as much a child of nature as the Bantus, and so exceeded them in physical and mental exploits, that for thirty years he had been unquestioned patriarch of the tribe.

More than once he had thought of reaching the Congo River and civilization but the Zulus roamed the lands between and the ever-present threat of attack aroused his fighting instinct. He trained the Bantus in simple warfare, and the Zulus came to respect his tribe which, though equipped with only bone and flint weapons, fought like demons.

So had Dan Williams spent a lifetime in Africa.

Then had come an echo from the dim past. A lone white man and his native *safari* had come, had embraced him and called him "cousin." And gradually Dan Williams had recognized his strange words.

Earl Hackworth had made three efforts in those forty years to find out what had happened to his uncle and cousin. His third had succeeded only after discovering a route free of the Zulu menace.

Hackworth had found his cousin to be a tall and amazingly strong man whose elastic step and youthful poise belied his fifty-eight years. Despite a dark-brown skin, scraggly bleached hair, and unkempt beard, Dan Williams was virile and sternly handsome.

Overjoyed, Hackworth had planned an immediate return, Williams, hesitant at first, finally agreed. But all during the three weeks' crossing of the jungles and wastes, he had been moody and taciturn. The truth was that Williams had been in a bewildered dream until that cry of "Dan" had recalled forgotten things.

And with that word had Dan Williams' forty years in the Dark Continent become just an interlude.

When they were within a mile of the ship, two black dots near the sirship waved.

"My armed guards," exclaimed Hackworth.

Though he had landed in the valley, hidden from view of the wasteland, he had taken no chance that wandering natives might damage or plunder the ship.

They reached it as evening shadows began to crawl across the valley floor. Before the sudden tropical darkness had overtaken them, they had stored most of their supplies in the roomy hold.

"We'll start at daybreak," Hackworth shouted to the natives. "Have anything you please for supper tonight."

Dan Williams looked over the airplane with an interested eye. Compared to the craft he had known of forty years before, this one seemed a monstrous distortion. To him it seemed practically all wings. Two mighty engines were set at about the mid-point of each wing. From close up, it looked ungainly and ugly, yet from the ridge top it had looked graceful and light, like a poised dragon-fly ready to spring enthusiastically into the air.

"What makes it rise vertically?" he asked, in a slow, measured voice, for as yet English was laborious for him, his tongue having rolled off Bantu dialect for forty long years.

Hackworth chuckled. "Well, Dan, this is a 1973 model. The wing design and draft deflectors are engineering developments never thought of forty years ago. They make it possible for a heavy all-metal ship like that to rise vertically. Without cutting engine speed, the pilot swings the engines horizontal when the ship has gained sufficient altitude."

"Do you own—the thing?" asked Williams.

"Sure."

"It looks expensive. You must have made a fortune. My father could never have gone on his exploration without the Belgian Government standing all expenses."

"I'll explain all that some other time," returned Hackworth with a short laugh. "By the way—that rawhide bundle of yours. If it has anything fragile in it, you'd better take it into the cabin. Otherwise I'll put it in the hold."

"In the cabin," said Williams quickly.

"And tomorrow," Hackworth went on, "you're going to get into civilized clothes. Those loin skins may look right to your Bantu friends, but not on the coast."

Williams looked down at his practically naked body, then raised amused eyes. "And I'm going to—to shave also."

They ate a delicious stew of meats and vegetables in the soft moonlit night, then crawled into Hackworth's tent.

# CHAPTER II

Williams found it hard to sleep. Tomorrow he would see civilization.

Forty years! How different would things be? What strange things had come to pass?

Africa. It was all around him, in the silvered shafts of moonlight. His mind visioned desert, wasteland, jungle, fertile river areas, the village of his simple Bantu friends. He murmured farewell.

"*Akka musri et graal umo*—farewell to my home that was."

In the dawn, the camp was quickly broken up and all stored away in the ship's hold.

The tall mulatto pilot Hackworth had hired at Kabinda, went busily about the ship, inspecting everything thoroughly.

Hackworth called the three Bantus from Williams' tribe who had accompanied the party. He handed them mirrors, combs, and colored beads, and as a gesture of great gratitude, presented a pair of binoculars to M'bopo.

M'bopo stared dumbly at the glasses.

"Good-by, M'bopo," said Williams in dialect. "May the spirits honor and cherish your prosperity in years to come."

Hackworth could detect the deep feeling between those two.

The wiry little soot-black man, whose sleek body fairly writhed with muscles, suddenly dashed the binoculars violently to the ground and the next moment was crying over and over, "*Umo ishta umi*—take me with you!"

Williams looked at Hackworth, his eyes moist, then exchanged several rapid phrases with M'bopo.

"He says that he wants to go with me even to the Seven Hills—Bantu for the end of space," Williams said. "Hackworth—"

Hackworth hesitated, thinking of a primitive man in the super-civilization of America. M'bopo's dark skin would not stand in his way—color prejudice had no great power in America now—but cultural differences… He sighed, then nodded.

"Plenty of room for him, Dan."

M'bopo leaped high into the air, turned his body around once, and slapped the soles of his feet together, all before landing again.

"He was the moon-dancer," explained Williams, seeing the astonishment in Hackworth's face. "Some of his acrobatic tricks would make you believe he was a wizard. We have been good friends. I'm not sorry he wants to come along."

Hackworth shouted for the men to board ship. Like a swarm of hornets, the natives scrambled into the ovoid. Plainly they considered the ride to the coast in an airplane the greatest of all great things. When they were all in, arranged on the benches by the pilot, the two Americans and M'bopo entered. Hackworth pointed to a bench facing the front window.

The cabin was roomy and bright. The soft woolen cushions on the benches were form-fitting and comfortable.

At a signal from Hackworth, the pilot moved his hands on the controls. The ship trembled and rose so gently that Williams saw the ground far below a moment later. Up and up it went as though pulled by some cosmic winch and chain. Then the tone beats of the engines changed as the pilot swung them to a horizontal pitch. With a pleasant surge, the airplane leaped forward. Below, the African topography blended into a flowing panorama.

Williams, peering around in fascination, muttered to himself in Bantu dialect. It might be days, weeks, or more, before he could be free of Africa and its subtle influence…

Hackworth paid off his *safari* men at Kabinda on the coast—a modern and important African port—and arranged to have his plane shipped to South America. He was a professional explorer, a vocation which had run in his and Dan's line for generations.

Obtaining passports for Williams and M'bopo at Kabinda, and attending to other matters took so much time that there was little chance for conversation, beyond talk of family affairs. Williams heard that the last remaining member of his family, his sister Helen, had died five years before.

Hackworth, and the explorer's daughter, were now Williams' closest relatives.

Hackworth bought tickets on the "hyp-marine" for quick passage to America. To Williams, at first glance, it had looked like a snub-nosed submarine, but with the difference that it had wings, short and stubby, at rear and front; along its upper length were spaced ten giant engine-housings; and there were thousands of tiny round spots running in lengthwise rows, gleaming with the iridescence of heavy glass.

When he first glimpsed it, it rested high and dry on a runway of rails at the end of the huge dock. In size it was much smaller than ocean liners he recalled.

With deepest interest Williams was surveying this craft that was to take them back to America when Hackworth stopped beside him smiling.

"Well, Dan, old boy," he said, "what do you think of the hyp-marine?"

"Wonderful," said Williams, looking down at the tumbled ocean surface. "But it doesn't have any decks. I don't like the idea of being cooped up in one little room for several days. Give me ocean liners with a promenade deck where one can breathe fresh salt air."

Hackworth smiled again. "Several days? Dan, we'll be in New York in twenty hours! You forget this is nineteen seventy-three. Our speed, constant and unvarying, is three hundred miles an hour."

"Impossible!" spluttered Williams. "Six thousand miles in twenty hours?"

"What would you say if I told you it is possible to cross from Europe to America in *two* hours, by means of stratosphere rocket ships?" Hackworth laughed at the startled expression in Williams' face. "Why, Dan, the three hundred miles an hour this hyp-marine makes is nothing these days for speed. There were many test flights, even back twenty years ago, when that speed was doubled—or more."

Williams relapsed into amazed silence.

The departure from port was a great thrill for Williams and his Bantu friend. First, the deep hum of air engines, gradually climbing the harmonic scale. Then the ship slid along the runway. There was a sinking sensation and the sound of lapping water, followed by a deep-throated roar from above.

For minutes, the ship swayed and rocked. Then gradually smoothness came, and Williams saw the ocean surface recede until not even the highest waves touched them. In a half-hour, the motion of the craft became uniform, and the noise above became a muffled drone. At the constant height of a hundred feet above water level, the hyp-marine skimmed the ocean like a preying gull.

The ship's interior ran in lengthwise tiers, five rows of rooms with corridors in between. The price for a room against the hull, and therefore having a round window for viewing seascapes, was double that of any interior room. But in comfort and elegance the rooms were uniform.

Hackworth and his two companions had a room for three, with three beds, three leather seats, sundry decorative articles, and a mirror. In this mirror, Williams had surveyed himself in surprise. Clean-shaven and scrupulously clean, he did not look at all like the wild image he had seen reflected in still African pools. His fine straw-yellow hair set off his healthy tan and sturdy features handsomely. Not one in a million would guess his age; he was a man in his prime, and felt that way.

Clothing styles had not changed much with men, except that closed collars had disappeared. The suit that Hackworth had helped him purchase at Kabinda was open-necked, a dull red. M'bopo had been outfitted with a soft green. Hackworth was wearing a suit of sky blue. Williams had noticed that all the men at Kabinda had worn colorful clothing.

M'bopo quickly proved adaptable. His eyes were constantly rolling in wonder but his features were inscrutable. He was as silent as an English butler, and not in the least troublesome. For him it was enough that "Orno Akku" (The White Orphan) was near him.

They had several meals in the huge public dining cabin, and for the rest of the time were glad to sleep. The trek through steamy, miasmic jungle had sapped their strength.

About an hour after they had left port Williams turned from the window to face Hackworth, who was undressing for bed. That morning, in Kabinda, Hackworth had received a radiogram. Reading it, he had contracted his brows fiercely, then without a word hastily stuffed the message away. Williams had wondered, for he had seen Hackworth's worry which now had grown deeper.

"Something is bothering you, Earl," Williams said. "That radiogram?"

Hackworth's face became suddenly haggard. "Oh, just something personal, Dan."

Their eyes met. "Wouldn't it be better if you unburdened your-self?" Williams asked quietly.

Hackworth hesitated, then motioned to chairs. They sat down.

"Dan, I've told you I have a daughter," said Hackworth, "a lovely girl of twenty. The radiogram was from her. What we've most dread-ed has finally happened. She had been summoned by the Unidum to marry a man she has never met and she—she loves another man."

"Unidum?" queried Williams perplexed. "Marry a man she has never met?"

Hackworth looked out at the limitless sweep of ocean and sky. "I see I'll have to do a little explaining, Dan. Our government today, the Unidum, is a sort of combination democracy and dictatorship, with a capital in New York City—"

"*Sarto je Bru!*" Williams burst out, with a Bantu curse. "What has become of our Constitution, of Congress and—"

"Later, Dan," said Hackworth, waving a hand. "Right now just remember there is a new regime under the Unidum. This ruling body made a national law ten years ago requiring all women to undergo eugenics tests before marriage. If the tests show the woman to fall into a certain genetic class, she is conscripted to become the mate of a scientist, for their children will have unusual intelligence, and will become scientists themselves!"

Astonishment and anger darkened the listening man's face.

"Lila—my daughter—met a young man named Terry Spath—a splendid chemist," Hackworth went on, "and they fell in love. I ap-proved of him and hoped to see them married. They would have been happy." Hackworth sighed heavily. "Lila took the unavoidable pre-marriage test a month ago. She wanted to have it over with and marry young Spath. There are really few women who prove fit and are con-scripted, but now this had to happen!"

He buried his face in his hands.

Williams was horrified. "When must Lila leave home?"

"She'll be gone when we get there," said Hackworth. "The Uni-dum is strict—and inexorable."

"Heartless, I'd say!" declared Williams. "Is there any way we can get to her before she is out of our reach entirely?"

"Well, yes."

Hackworth pulled out the radiogram and glanced at it.

"She will be at a downtown air terminal for a half-hour after we arrive in New York. But what's the idea, Dan?"

"If we can catch Lila in time, she will not become an unwilling bride!"

Hackworth looked at his cousin with narrowed eyes. "Impossible!"

"Earl," Williams said firmly, "your daughter's future and happiness are at stake. Are you willing to gamble for her sake?"

Hackworth looked at his cousin searchingly. Williams seemed to radiate a quiet assurance, this man who ruled a tribe of natives in the Congo. The distraught Hackworth nodded for him to go on.

"I have in my rawhide bundle," said Williams, "a vegetable drug—a rather remarkable one. D'Lawoef, the sole survivor of the expedition before ours, was a physiologist. His purpose in penetrating to that wild region was to procure a fair supply of this drug. During the eight years he lived there before we arrived, he collected quite a supply of the plant. He ground it up after drying it into a flake form, always in the hope that some day he would again reach civilization. Before he died, he confided in my father and me and turned his supply over to us. After father died this disappeared, all except one small clay box of it, which I have in my rawhide bundle."

Hackworth waited silently, wondering what all this would lead to.

"The alcoholic extraction of this vegetable," Williams went on, "has remarkable properties, according to D'Lawoef. Injected into the veins, it puts a person into a comatose condition for a long period of time, depending on the dose. The subject suffers no harm provided nourishment is given, like that given patients with sleeping sickness, either sugar in the veins, or simple liquid food."

Hackworth suddenly saw the significance. "Then you suggest that Lila be given the drug and—"

"And her marriage to the scientist forestalled. After that, we can plan what to do."

The hope in Hackworth's face was suddenly replaced by despair. "But the Unidum! They will send investigators. Suspicion will be directed at us—"

"Are you even afraid to gamble? This Unidum—you talk as if it were a king and you its abject slave! Forty years ago people did not cringe to government, especially when it was in the wrong. And this eugenics business is certainly tyrannically applied... Well, Earl, shall we use the drug, or let Lila be married with a broken heart?"

"It's worth the chance!" cried Hackworth, springing to his feet. Abruptly he added, "But the drug might be dangerous! What assurance have we, beyond D'Lawoef's word, that it is not harmful? It might poison Lila, cripple her, derange her mind!" Williams leaped to his feet and paced the room. He was willing to trust D'Lawoef's word, having known the man. But Hackworth would naturally be apprehensive about letting his daughter be drugged by a substance unknown and untried.

Suddenly Williams whirled. "Young Terry is a chemist, isn't he? We'll put the whole matter before him, let him test the drug some way, and make the final decision. After all, he is more vitally concerned than either you or I."

"If Terry approves," cried Hackworth, his face lighting up again with hope. "I can have no further objections."

With a great load off his mind, Hackworth began again to undress.

"Can we get a message to Terry?" asked Williams. "Time is precious. There will be little enough of it after we dock. We must have him prepared."

Hackworth looked dubious. "Radiograms are carefully looked over by Unidum officials. If we even mentioned Lila's name immediate investigation might start. They would apprehend us on the dot. However, we *could* send him an urgent message asking him to meet us."

"Get that message through," said Williams...

Two hours before the hyp-marine was due at the New York docks, when they were thoroughly rested and wide-awake, Williams asked Hackworth to explain the mysterious Unidum more fully.

Hackworth went into explanation directly. "In nineteen fifty-three, a great war which for some time had been brewing, broke out in Europe, after the one aggressor state left there had made stupendous preparations for it in the matter of huge tanks, guns, ordinary bombs, rockets and other armaments, with that boastful state confident of eventual world domination. Already that state had conquered other smaller states within its near orbit, had made them satellites and armed them. China had been overrun, and war had been brought to other Eastern countries, like Korea, which had involved our own country as well as other states in Europe.

"It was called the All-Nations War, and cataclysmic battles quickly brought in every nation in the world to greater or lesser degree. It was World War One and World War Two all over again—neither of which concerned people in deepest Africa—but ten times more hideous. The nation which started the holocaust had not fully realized the devastation of the atomic bomb, although that had been horribly demonstrated on Hiroshima and Nagasaki when Japan was defeated at the supposed close of World War Two. Japan had brought the United States into the conflict by a sneak bombing attack on Pearl Harbor, in December nineteen forty-one. World War Two was started by a psychopathic genius named Hitler, in nineteen thirty-nine..."

Williams was looking perplexed.

"You've actually heard of Hitler, Dan. He was the leader of a small but fanatical party in Germany, and he became Chancellor in nineteen thirty-three, not long before you left for Africa. Everyone thought that he had been buried—the way people thought that Teddy Roosevelt was safely out of the running when he was elected Vice President. Well, they were wrong both times. Hitler maneuvered himself into dictatorial power and built up a tremendous military machine in Germany, while the nations which could have stopped him refused to take him seriously. England, France, and America were virtually disarmed. Russia was isolated. Japan and Italy allied themselves with Germany, and the Japanese gobbled up China piecemeal while Hitler was making bloodless conquests in Europe by blackmail and bluff, preparing for all-out war."

Williams nodded slowly. "Then this A-bomb... our side had it? What is it?"

"I'll try to explain it to you later. The United States and Germany were both working on it, but we managed to get it first. Once it was used, there couldn't be any such thing as effective secrecy, so other nations developed it, too. But in the All-Nations War, a still more deadly missile, the hydrogen bomb, made its appearance—and if there had been a long enough time for development, a longer period of uneasy peace with all nations building up armaments, the H-bomb might have written finis to humanity. As it was, Europe was soon a shambles, and this time America did not escape bombings. Hostilities finally ceased—it was a short war with no winners, as scientists had predicted when nuclear weapons appeared—and a titanic revolution broke out in the United States, ending with the rise of the Unidum.

"You've heard of it before, too, Dan. It came out of what was called Technocracy when we were young. A group of scientists and technicians, economic philosophers, educators, etc., foreseeing the probabilities, had banded together in preparation. It pushed over staggering governments, set up its own, and brought reason and order out of chaos. The Unidum came into being in nineteen fifty-four as the central government of all Europe and North America. Asia formed a federation under a ruling central power, while Africa and South America formed unit federations.

"The Unidum capital is in New York City, once the headquarters of the United Nations, a body formed after World War Two, supposedly for arbitration and the prevention of wars. After its downfall the Unidum took over, and from that city now guides the collective destiny of a half-billion souls."

Williams whistled in amazement. "How is it possible to hold under one rule so many different peoples, each with a different language, and many who are hereditary enemies?"

Hackworth smiled. "Because, Dan, the Unidum is composed of intellectual giants whose methods are clever and admirably efficient. The English language became standard in all Unitaria, which is the name for our country; and work was divided wisely and with justice.

"And so, Dan," summarized Hackworth, drawing a long breath, "things are now vastly different from forty years ago politically. There was co-operation all over Unitaria when one language became standard and all people had the same privileges and rights, even the sad remnants of the original aggressor nations. In Europe, Dan, the Unitaria-fostered brotherhood had been a few dozen states, each speaking a different language and each jealous of the other, though it was only the traditions of centuries that had kept antagonism alive. Once the Unidum stepped in and painted out boundaries and made them responsible to Unitaria as a whole, those old prejudices could begin to evaporate, and many of the worst have disappeared in two decades."

Dan had listened, incredulous.

"It all sounds nice enough, Earl. I can hardly credit the same Unidum with passing a law like the one that affects Lila."

Hackworth lowered his voice.

"Naturally, this is no millennium or Utopia. The scientists, who now have a finger in government, are stony-hearted in their zeal for a better world. The Eugenics Law is an example of that."

They fell silent. Hackworth was again worried, and Williams was finding it strange that his return to civilization had precipitated him immediately against law and order—at least one phase of it…

An hour later, Williams looked out to see a strange new world. The Statue of Liberty was still there but the New York skyline was incredibly changed. Buildings had sprouted amazingly with spiderlike spans and vines. It was feverishly unreal. And what were those bees and flies swarming around?

Williams started at a sharp nudge in his ribs.

"Come out of it, man!" Hackworth said.

When they stepped onto the dock, Williams was clutching his rawhide bundle tightly. The customs and passports inspection were rapid and efficient; they were quickly released.

While Williams was staring at the colorful crowds a tall young man immediately strode up to them.

"Terry, my boy!" cried Hackworth. "How are you?"

"Fine. But you—Africa hasn't treated you so well. You are thinner!"

"There are other things," muttered Hackworth. He then presented Williams and M'bopo.

Terry Spath was a tall, ruggedly handsome young man of twenty-four, with a splendid muscular development. His calm gray eyes might hide lurking fires. The determined line of his mouth and chin bespoke a sturdy will.

After the introductions, immediately Hackworth looked grave again. Terry touched his arm. "You still have time to—to see Lila, if we all hurry."

"We *must* see her, must *stop* her!" returned Hackworth.

Terry opened his eyes wide. "But the summons! If we stop her, the Unidum guards will come after her!"

"We're wasting time," said Williams fiercely. "Let's go after Lila and explain later. You and I, Earl, will go. You, Terry, and M'bopo must go to your laboratory." He pulled from his pocket a crude clay box. "Make any tests you can of the alcoholic extraction of the vegetable fiber in this box. *Everything depends on that!*"

Williams flung a rapid flood of dialect at M'bopo while Hackworth gave Terry a hurried explanation of the intended use of the drug.

"Bring her back, then!" cried Terry, and the lurking fires in his eyes flashed to sudden life.

There was a man with spirit, reflected Williams, as he and Hackworth took an escalator to the electro-car station.

To Williams it was all confusion and madness, this New York of 1973, strange, incredible. Bright clothes, great crowds, voices, droning loudspeakers. Yet how subdued was the city noise! The old crashes and bangs and shrill whistles were gone. And where was traffic? He could see none on the ground there… *Sarto*! That wasn't the ground! They were on a sort of aerial highway. Those bees and flies were aircraft!

Hackworth was pointing to an open door on a long, wide enclosed platform. There were comfortable seats inside. They sat down. Williams started as two semi-flexible bands seemed to jump out of nowhere and enfold his thighs and lower chest.

A low whine sobbed through the air. A slight jerk. A feeling of pressure. Past the windows a blur of striated metal swept. Brief glimpses came to Williams from the window of bottomless chasms and leaning heights.

There was a swift stop, a complete swing, then more motion that must be blinding speed. "*Je Bru il Bra!*" thought Williams. Forty years of Africa had certainly not prepared him for this supercivilization!

Suddenly he saw Hackworth on his feet and started to jump up, only to find the thigh and chest bands holding him back. Hackworth pressed on the elbow rest with his hand. The stiff bands swung back. They stepped out on a platform, again enclosed like an island in space. Escalators—down to a wide level space that seemed to be the flat roof of a building.

"The air terminal," informed Hackworth.

The level space was a landing field. As they traversed a pedestrian walk bounded by latticework rails, a humming monster fell from the sky not a hundred yards away—a sudden roar of propellers, then people stepped out calm and indifferent.

Hackworth pointed to a huge clock.

"We've got five minutes to find Lila!"

An elevator took them below to the loading platform depot for passengers. Hurried questions to "Information," then Hackworth raced toward the numbered air-liner berths. People were milling, entering the giant flying wing with four engines.

Hackworth frantically searched the crowd. His lips were unconsciously saying "Lila! Lila!" Then he ran forward.

"Lila!"

A girl with magnificent auburn hair turned. Her eyes caught theirs and she stood stock-still. Hackworth ran to her eagerly and embraced her.

"I'm so glad you got here in time to see me before—" Williams heard Lila say.

"Not just to see you," said Hackworth. He looked around nervously. "But to take you back home!"

"Why… Oh, no! The summons! I must hurry—the ship leaves in a few minutes."

Hackworth gently pulled her to the wall where the crowd was thin.

"Lila, dear, you're coming with us. Dan Williams here—"

In great surprise Lila extended her hand and flashed him a smile.

"Dan," went on Hackworth in a rapid whisper, "wants you to let him help us all. We've met Terry already—he's waiting."

The girl's face reflected astonishment and indecision. "But, Father, I must go. I've had three summonses already! They threatened to send guards if I failed to arrive."

"Lila," said Williams, "will you trust me that I can help you and Terry?"

Their eyes met, sturdy blue and limpid brown. Something seemed to emanate from the blue eyes, something that could be trusted.

"Yes, Mr. Williams."

"Lead the way," Williams said quickly to Hackworth. "Terry's laboratory."

# CHAPTER III

An electro-car took them to the suburban plant of the food products Branch E, where Terry worked as a chemist. Williams was surprised that suburban New York had hardly changed at all in comparison to the downtown business section. It looked familiar here.

When they descended to the street level he saw pavements and residences, such as he had seen when he was eighteen. But he merely had to look up at the electro-car gathering tremendous speed, a long silver needle in the distance, to realize that it was 1973.

Hackworth led the way to the long, low plant and opened the door. They passed down a long hallway and stopped before a closed door where Hackworth knocked.

Terry's voice came to them. "Come in."

He was standing before a bench covered with glassware and bottled materials. In his rubber-gloved hand he held a test-tube half filled with a delicate green solution.

Terry turned, and his eyes lighted as he went toward Lila with outstretched arms. They clung to each other mutely. Williams quietly closed the door and turned a key in the lock. Terry had been alone in the room, and secrecy was vital.

"Terry," said Lila, gently extricating herself from his arms, "why are we all here in your laboratory?"

"I hardly know myself. Mr. Williams—"

Hackworth interrupted. "I'll explain. Dan conceived a plan for keeping Lila from being married to a Unidum scientist and convinced me that it was worth a trial. But the final decision rests between you and Lila, Terry. Dan, tell about the drug."

Williams pointed to the opened clay box on the bench, half-filled with a dry, flaky material like rough-cut tobacco.

"What did you find out about it?" he asked Terry.

"Well, the time has been short and the tests simple, but it is related to narcotics like opium and morphine. It should produce a sleep state.

But it has a reaction that puzzles me. Is it widely distributed in Africa, Mr. Williams?"

"No. The man who collected that vegetable flake told me that it is a rare plant, existing only in central Congo. He planned to carry a lot of it back to civilization and test its narcotic principle. His name was D'Lawoef."

"D'Lawoef!" echoed Terry excitedly. "Well-known physiologist of two generations ago! Did he tell you anything more?"

"He said it would produce a comatose state in any living being for periods of time depending on the dose," said Williams. "Not a dream state or semi-consciousness like opium, but complete repose. There is no common antidote according to D'Lawoef. He knew that because he tried it on a native and failed to rouse him. He believed that probably there is no antidote, for it is a remarkable substance."

Terry nodded. He held up a small flask holding a colorless liquid.

"Here it is in a ten-to-one alcohol and water solution—ready for injection!"

So Terry would not hesitate to take the gamble! But Lila? Her eyes showed bewilderment.

"Lila," Williams said, "an injection of that liquid will put you into a coma or induced sleep. Then we will inform the Unidum that you are strangely unconscious and cannot therefore be married. What they will do we can't say, but it will prevent your forced marriage. After that, we will see if that can be turned aside altogether."

"Oh, I—I don't dare!" she said. She added quickly, "Not because I'm afraid for myself, but because the Unidum will make things miserable for you three." The men looked at one another.

"For our love's sake, take it, Lila!" Terry urged. "If the Unidum does find out, I'll take the blame! It must be my responsibility. Lila, darling, take the drug! It may bring us together in the future!"

Lila threw herself into his arms in consent.

"When will the Unidum begin finding out that Lila had disobeyed the summons?" asked Williams.

"Possibly tonight. The summons demanded Lila's appearance at the Unidum Sub-Headquarters in Philadelphia before eight P.M. By nine or ten, they will begin to lose patience."

"It's now six," said Williams, while the others waited, unconsciously accepting his leadership. The same dominance in his character that had made him chieftain and sole ruler of a thousand natives in Africa was making itself felt.

"We'll all go to your home now, Earl," he said tersely. "We'll give Lila the drug, then wait for the authorities to make the next move."

"I have my car outside," said Terry.

Terry made a package of the solution and a hypodermic needle, locking the rest of the vegetable fiber in a cabinet. They left the laboratory, and M'bopo followed them silently.

Terry opened the door of a sleek, satin-finished automobile whose long body seemed to flow in ripples from a blunt rear apex. To Williams it looked like the futuristic advertisements of forty years ago come true. The smooth purr of a powerful motor was uninterrupted by shifting gears as the vehicle glided forward with magical ease.

During the half-hour drive from the laboratory to the Hackworth home, little was said. Their nerves were tense. Williams took in the passing scenery with an eager eye. Change—change. Forty years of it, a lifetime of it. Yet here and there some sections were startlingly familiar. Pedestrians walked leisurely, even indolently. The tempo of city life had apparently decreased. Even the cars, except theirs, crawled along as though the drivers had all the time in the world.

Finally they entered a section of tree-shaded avenues lined with bungalows and small mansions. The dwellings were spaced widely and exhibited individual styles. At least 1973 had brought something invigorating in residential architecture. Stereotyped standards had been abolished.

Terry halted the car before a small, neat bungalow surrounded by hedges, flower patches, and wide lawns.

The interior was luxurious, almost lavish, but homelike. The furniture was a blend of elegance and comfort. A manservant took the suitcases.

Dinner was immediately served, and Lila displayed her sparkling spirit during the meal, despite the chill thought of what would transpire later.

Williams ate mechanically, deep in thought. At the end of the meal, he suddenly looked up and said, "There's something more about the drug I haven't mentioned."

"Let's all go into the living room," put in Hackworth.

When they had made themselves comfortable, Williams said, "D'Lawoef mentioned that he had found the natives using the drug.

The medicine men use it to induce restful sleep in fevers and painful sicknesses. The Frenchman also claimed that the person under the influence of the drug could be made to respond to impressions given just before the coma overtook him—something like hypnotism, I suppose. If we could be sure of that we could impress on Lila's brain the suggestion not to awaken until somebody's voice, Terry's preferably, commanded her to!"

"But what would be the purpose of that?" queried Terry.

"In case the Unidum sends doctors to revive her—doctors who might succeed. But the hypnosis ought to last longer than the drug, according to D'Lawoef."

"But how can we test that now?" asked Hackworth. "Time is getting short—a quarter to eight!" Williams shifted his eyes to M'bopo who sat cross-legged on the rug, and spoke softly in Bantu dialect. The man's expression became frightened. Sharp words changed it to resignation. M'bopo muttered, and bowed his head.

"M'bopo is my assistant and friend. I could not order him to do this, but he would not refuse an appeal. We have saved each other's lives more than once, and I would take no less risk for his sake," Williams informed them. "Get the hypodermic, Terry. Give him the smallest dose conceivable."

Terry opened his package in which was a sterilizing solution as well as the drug and hypodermic. He dipped the needle, wiped it with cotton, and drew in a drop. M'bopo bared his arm. Terry plunged the needle in and pushed the plunger.

Immediately Williams waved him back and began to speak slowly and emphatically in dialect, gazing into the man's eyes. The other's watched intently.

A film came over M'bopo's eyes and they dropped shut. Williams caught his tumbling body and set it in a chair.

"That small dose ought to be ineffective in fifteen minutes," he said. "Then we'll see."

* * * *

When the clock struck eight, Williams asked Hackworth to shake M'bopo and command him in dialect to awake. But no amount of shaking or talking brought any change to the senseless African. Then Williams motioned his cousin away.

"*Umo gaak*, M'bopo!"

The eyelids fluttered and flicked open. M'bopo looked up with a sigh of relief.

"Then it works!" cried Terry.

"Not conclusively," amended Williams. "The dose might have been just enough to keep him asleep until after Hackworth tried to awaken him. But it gives us a reasonable hope that Lila can be put into a coma from which only one person can awaken her—Terry. So—"

At a clicking sound echoing through the room, Williams stopped.

"The Unidum radio signal!" cried Hackworth. "It is more than likely about Lila!"

"Then listen," Williams said rapidly. "Lila is strangely sick, has been in a coma for the past few hours. You are about to call a doctor."

Hackworth placed himself before a projecting mouthpiece in the wall, surrounded by a carved frame of gilt metal. He tripped one of two levers beside it, which would throw the incoming voice through the room; the other lever would have brought the voice through a receiver hanging on a hook just below the mouthpiece—for private conversations.

"Hackworth speaking."

"Unidum calling. Eugenics Bureau." The voice was peremptory, commanding. "Your daughter Lila has failed to appear at the sub-headquarters in Philadelphia, as specified in the third and final summons of three days ago. What have you to say?"

"I am sorry. I—I—"

Williams gripped his cousin's hand tightly. Hackworth spoke more firmly.

"My daughter has inexplicably—er—become ill this afternoon. She is in a coma and nothing seems to awaken her."

"What?" came sternly from the diaphragm on the wall. "Is this some trick?"

"No," said Hackworth, playing his part with more assurance. "My daughter has not been well for days. She simply collapsed and has failed to awaken."

"Have you a doctor?"

"No, but I was just going to—"

"Never mind," interrupted the voice. "We will send our choice of doctors, since your daughter is legally under the authority of the Unidum's Bureau of Eugenics." A click and the voice was gone.

Hackworth wiped a perspiring brow.

"You see, Williams, what the Unidum is like? There'll be a doctor from them here inside of an hour. He will—"

"We must hurry," interrupted Williams. He looked into the girl's eyes and said, "Lila, are you ready?"

Without a word, she kissed Terry, then bared her arm. Terry filled the hypodermic needle and slowly brought it closer to her arm, trembling in every limb. Lila caught his eye and silently commanded him to go ahead.

Then it was done, and Terry was holding her close, looking into her eyes, was saying over and over, "Wake up only at my command, darling…"

Three days after Lila Hackworth had been given the mysterious narcotic, Dan Williams sat before a two-foot oval screen in his cousin's home with the shades down so that the television images would be clear. M'bopo sat beside him, the whites of his eyes gleaming eerily in the ghost-light of faintly illuminated dial controls.

Talking and singing figures became involved in a stirring intrigue of the year in which the rising Unidum regime had startled a whole world. The sound effects which seemed to come from every corner of the room were perfection.

When the drama ended, Williams brought to the screen a race between a rocket auto and a rocket train on tracks. He was awed when the announcer revealed that the event was taking place at that identical moment near Berlin, for television had been but in its infancy in 1933, and stereophony a dream.

The front door slammed and Hackworth came in.

"That drug is all you said it was, Dan," he declared. "Lila is sleeping as sweetly as a child. The doctors are stumped. They asked me a hundred questions and I kept looking heartbroken. It was great!" He seemed in great good humor.

"Did they seem suspicious?" asked Williams.

"Well, when I mentioned having just returned from Africa, the three doctors looked at each other significantly. I know what they figured. Sleeping sickness! Transmitted from me as a passive carrier. They'll work at that angle, and get more puzzled. Dan, my heart sank the other night when the Unidum doctor ordered Lila removed to the Eugenics Bureau's own hospital. I thought sure they would waken her, but now—"

"D'Lawoef was right after all, Earl. Is she in good hands—being fed properly, and so on?"

"The Unidum doctors and hospitals are the pride of medical science, Dan. They'll take perfect care of her."

"The next move," said Williams, "will be ours. Terry will be here tonight. We'll talk it over then. Right now, suppose you tell me a few things I haven't had a chance to find out. Up until now it's been hustle and bustle and rush and run. I have only the vaguest idea of what sort of world I'm living in."

"Come into the living room," said Hackworth.

# CHAPTER IV

Passing through the lounge on the way to the living room, Williams and Hackworth found M'bopo twisting the television dials and staring at the screen in fascination. Williams grinned at him and told him to play the set all he wanted to. He went on with his cousin.

"First of all," said Williams when they were seated in the living room and had lighted cigars, "tell me about yourself, Earl. We've been together for days and I still don't know what your life has been in the past forty years or how you came to find me in the heart of Africa."

"Well," said Hackworth, "exploration has occupied most of my life. It runs in the family. In the All-Nations War I was an officer in the United States Air Force and, God help me, I have seen too many people, Dan, exterminated like rats in minutes."

He passed a hand across his eyes and shuddered.

"I'm trying to forget that war—I never can! I was a surveyor for new sites for cities in America. Millions were shipped over from starving, exhausted Europe and put to work in the new cities.

"That was the beginning of reconstruction—postwar rejuvenation. When my requests were finally granted I was commissioned an explorer. I've been in dozens of out-of-the-way corners of the world. I married, but my wife died in bearing Lila.

"One thing you must know, Dan—I never forgot you and your father. But knowing Africa as you do, especially the Congo—but *not* knowing the Unidum Exploration Bureau—you may not understand why I tried to reach you only twice, and twice failed. Three years ago I discovered a rich deposit of platinum ores in Siberia. My rewards made me independent, so I was able to search for a north route, and finally penetrated to you. I had little hope of seeing any of your father's expedition alive, so you may imagine my joy when I saw a white man and learned it was you.

"That's my life, Dan. I could sit the rest of my days in an armchair, if I wanted to. But I'm planning on trying the Amazon again now."

Williams smiled. "I understand. The fire in your blood that has been in the Williams line since the discovery of America, the same urge that sent my father and myself into the Congo forty years ago." He grew thoughtful. "Speaking of wealth, Earl, is there as much unrest between labor and management today as there used to be?"

Hackworth shrugged. "There is no such thing as complete private ownership of industry today, yet we have avoided the evils of outright socialism. Incentive remains, and consumer demand plays its part in the economy. But neither labor nor capital have overwhelming power. The Unidum controls transportation, communication, and food. All other industries are under Unidum sponsorship, too, in a lesser degree. The average standard of living is high in Unitaria. Our 'rich' would have been considered paupers by the money barons of forty years ago, but our 'poor' never face want nor privation."

Williams was surprised. "Then the Unidum has done good work."

"Yes, Dan, perhaps more good than evil. But there are sad mistakes made, like the Eugenics Law. Still the basic idea of that law is worthy."

"But forcing women into loveless marriages is inhuman!" protested Williams.

"Sacrifice of personal happiness for future benefits to the state is a choice many men and women have made freely all through history. But requiring such sacrifices by law, in peacetime, is just what a dictator would think of! Earl, just how do those scientists figure in the Unidum?"

"Well, the term 'scientist' is applied only to a person of knowledge who has proved himself. I say 'himself' for simplicity's sake, but there's no sex discrimination. Usually he must perform some brilliant intellectual work, for which he receives the special privileges accorded men of science. The Unidum is composed of two equal-powered executives, two lawmaking bodies, two judicial systems, and a long line of bureaus. One-half of the government is in the hands of scientists. One of the executives is a scientist, one of the legislative bodies is the House of Scientists, one of the judicial systems is the Science Court, and many of the Bureaus are purely scientific in nature—as the Eugenics Bureau."

"And the resulting government?"

"Has made Unitaria a supercivilization. For the first time in history, the intellectual forces have become the governing power. In the past, it had always been the ruthless, hereditary, and selfish forces. The Unidum is the first experiment in a rule of *reason* as opposed to a rule of *might*."

"But the Eugenics Law," said Williams. "There is no justification for that."

Hackworth waved a hand noncommittally. "Enough for a while," he said. "It's dinner time." Terry arrived after dinner. Hackworth told him what had occurred at the hospital.

"By the way," he said hesitantly, "I met the scientist that Lila— er—was to have married. Professor Jorgen, a biologist. He was nice enough, except for his overbearing air of self-importance—something Lila could never have endured. He assured me he would do all in his power to see that she was cured. He was all confidence."

Terry's lips tightened. "The very thought of any man touching her while she lies helpless—"

"I know how you feel, Terry," interrupted Hackworth. "I'm glad I didn't take you along, though, for you'd have been sure to get into trouble."

"Professor Jorgen," said Terry, frowning darkly. "I'll make him wish he'd never heard of Lila Hackworth."

"But the Unidum would make you wish you'd never met Jorgen," Hackworth said drily. "Besides, you know perfectly well that if anything happened to Jorgen, Lila would be given to another scientist."

"Just a minute," Williams said firmly. "We want to plan for the future, not discuss violence. Now, in brief, Lila is lost to Terry under the Eugenics Law, but she is in such a state the Unidum cannot force her marriage to a scientist. We are reasonably sure she will not awaken till Terry himself commands her to, and she will be well taken care of. There are only two possibilities as I see it. Strings must be pulled to release Lila from the Eugenics Law, or she must be spirited away to a foreign land."

"The first is practically impossible," said Hackworth.

"Why?" countered Williams. "You have money, haven't you? You can bribe officials and buy out opposition."

"Once," Hackworth said, "bribery and graft were a flourishing trade. But the Unidum, with its ideals, is adamant to corruption. Money wouldn't take the dot off an 'i' in any Unidum records!"

"Are there any influential men who would help you for the sake of friendship?"

"Doubtful," muttered Hackworth.

"Would it do any good to appeal to a court?" Hackworth and Terry exchanged wan smiles.

"That would be like taking meat from a hungry lion and offering it dried biscuits," said Hackworth. "You see, Dan, most of the women confiscated by the Eugenics Law take it philosophically. They are treated well, their husbands are influential and respected—courts would laugh at the petition to grant one girl a release because she loves another man."

"Yet you, Earl, and Terry, *you* would not laugh."

"I should say not!" declared Terry vehemently. "I've never believed the Eugenics Law was right. Women should have a free choice."

"I agree heartily," said Hackworth.

"Well," said Williams, "since neither bribery nor friendship will release Lila, the only possibility left is—"

"Wait!" cried Hackworth suddenly. "I have a close friend in Long Island who might... At least I can talk to him about it. He is secretary to Executive Ashley."

"Who?"

"One of the two executives of the Unidum, corresponding to the president of a democracy. The scientist executive is Professor Molier. Ashley, the other, is not a scientist."

"That's worth a trial," said Williams.

"We can't bank on it too much," Hackworth added gloomily. "Dan, you have no idea of the efficiency and—and impregnability of the Unidum."

"You've said that before," drawled Williams. "But I, for one, will battle the whole iron system for Lila's sake. We've halted the Unidum decree for a time. Why lose heart?"

"I'm with you!" cried Terry.

"And so am I," said Hackworth.

"In Africa," said Williams, "when surrounded by Zulus, I hunted until I found a weak point. Then I sent through a body of my best Bantu warriors to fall on their backs. More than once we beat off an enemy five times our strength. We must find the Unidum's weak point, if any. If not, we must resort to flight.

"Terry, just go about your work until you get a call from us..."

The airport where Hackworth kept another private Sansrun plane was a mile from his home. On a warm and pleasant September day,

Hackworth, Williams, and M'bopo walked toward it. Now and then an automobile purred smoothly by, shining in the bright sun. Overhead an occasional plane droned alone. Far to the left sped an electro-car like an enlarged needle.

"Somehow," said Williams, "this just seems like nineteen thirty-three caricatured by a clever artist. I can still see the old city behind all this. Maybe I was dreaming when I stepped from the hyp-marine and thought I saw Manhattan Island overgrown with a strange architecture."

Hackworth smiled. "Downtown has been almost completely re-built, but the rest of New York has stayed pretty much the same. The same has happened in all big cities of Unitaria. Similarly, complete though the change has been in government and state affairs, social life has not changed to a great extent. People still play and sing and gossip. There are still theaters, movies, parties, banquets, and idle recreation—perhaps too much of that with the short working week. We still have our foibles, pet peeves, petty faults, and idiosyncrasies. Forty years has not changed human nature."

The airport was small, but Hackworth explained that it was only one of hundreds spread through the residence sections for private craft.

Then Hackworth's ship came from the hangar, a fair-sized one with twin motors. They climbed into it. Its front was of flawless glass. The controls, rear fins and all, were embodied in a driving wheel and foot throttle.

Hackworth took altitude with the carelessness of experience. At a thousand feet, he tripped a small lever on the control panel.

To their ears came a faint staccato tapping above the muffled engine buzz. Hackworth swung to one side until the noise became louder and less shrill. Suddenly there was a chorus of new sounds with a regular rhythm. He began a swift climb. Another series of fluted notes and he leveled out. At five thousand feet he relaxed.

"You see, Dan," he explained, "one must fly carefully around New York, or any big city. The air is divided into zones and lanes for different types of craft. Those sounds are lane signals. By means of them, an experienced flyer can fly with his eyes closed. They tell me what lane I'm in, where to turn, where to rise or descend and what speed limit to observe."

While in the lane, the noises went on regularly and not unpleasantly.

Hackworth pointed to striped ships that they passed at long intervals.

"Air-traffic police."

The traffic became heavy as they approached downtown New York. A steady stream of small Sansrun craft flowed by. A thousand feet up darted larger ships with multiple engines. High above in endless rows were passenger ships bound for, or returning to, distant cities. Hackworth made another ascent when the signals fluted, and leveled at nine thousand feet. From this viewpoint Williams could see a geometric pattern of air-traffic spread over New York like a fisher's shimmering net.

They followed a weaving course that circled them past the southern edge of downtown New York. From this height it looked more unreal than it had from the ground, Williams reflected. He had a mental picture of 1933 New York in his mind, which he compared with what his eyes saw in 1973. Downtown crawled inward considerably, had become less spired, and had fallen victim of a Titanic spider which had spun an intricate web between the interstices of buildings.

Hackworth piloted the ship in the Long Island lane.

"The Unidum capitol," he said, pointing downward.

Williams gasped in sheer astonishment. On the western side of the East River was a large group of magnificent buildings of glass and shining metal, glittering in the sun with blinding intensity. They covered acres of ground, majestic structures that could have been touched with the inspired finger of a futuristic artist. It was a hive of activity, aircraft rising and descending, autos creeping like ants, and tiny dots entering and leaving the various buildings.

"So there is the place where the destiny of half a billion souls is centered," commented Williams. He suddenly realized forcefully just what a gargantuan state Unitaria was—the old United States, Canada, Mexico, then over to the Old World—Britain, Germany, Russia, others. It seemed impossible in scope.

Hackworth began to maneuver downward when they had passed the Unidum capitol. He sped the plane finally two thousand feet above ground. Long Island City clustered halfway between the two tips of its namesake island. It had been taken over simultaneously with the founding of the capitol and now was purely a residence city for the tens of thousands of Unidum employees. It had, therefore, been arranged with an eye for beauty. From the air it gave the impression of a sleepy Mid-western town that had grown to a city without changing its rural aspect. Thousands of picturesque bungalows and low apartment hotels dotted the carpet of lush green grass, and endless rows of trees lent it a quiet, woodland air.

# CHAPTER V

Landing at one of the small airports in Long Island City, Hackworth left the plane in charge of the hangar attendants. A half-mile walk down shady avenues brought them before a stucco dwelling.

Williams was introduced to the man who answered the doorbell—Andrew Grant, secretary to Executive Ashley of the Unidum. He was a short, slight man of fifty, bald and spectacled. His sonorous voice seemed out of keeping with his physique as he conducted his visitors to the lounge. Hackworth did not delay in coming to the point.

"Andrew," he said, "I've dropped in on you for a purpose."

Grant lifted bushy eyebrows.

"It's about Lila," said Hackworth. "She has taken the Eugenics Test and found to be the type needed."

"I was sorry when I heard that," said Grant quickly. "Lila is a wonderful girl. And young Terry—I suppose he's broken-hearted?"

"Naturally. None of us felt any too pleased about—" He paused, then said hastily: "Andrew, you will hold anything I say in utmost confidence?"

"Surely. You know me well enough for that."

"Well, Lila is in a condition preventing her marriage. While this *impasse* holds, young Terry Spath, Mr. Williams here, and I are going to try to save Lila from the Eugenics Law. I have come to you hoping you may be able to help."

Grant had suddenly turned grave. He looked hastily about. "What do you mean?"

"Isn't there any possible way to annul the Unidum decree?" asked Hackworth.

There was a pause before Grant answered. His eyes avoided his friend.

"Well—Earl, really it's unheard of! Unidum decrees are not subject to repeal. You should know that."

Hackworth threw a glance of helplessness at Williams. He heaved a weary sigh. "I know that, Andrew. But you can't blame me for trying. A father's heart prompts me. Suppose your daughter, Elaine, loved a young man and—" Grant's face suddenly paling checked him.

Grant came to his feet and paced up and down, then he whirled. "You're right, Earl," he said tensely. "Elaine will have to take the test soon. She has met a young man… That Eugenics Law—a thousand curses on it! I've always hated it, and you and I are not the only ones. It is one of the worst mistakes the Unidum has ever made. I'd like to help you, Earl, if… Is Lila ill?"

Hackworth told the whole story then, while the surprised Grant looked at Williams with a new interest. When Hackworth finished, Grant said, "I shall do my best to help Lila. I've got connections in the Unidum that may, or may not, result in her release. I'm not underestimating the task. As far as I know, no woman has ever been released from the Eugenics Law, but there is a first time for everything. Give me a week's time to do some guarded investigation."

"If only Lila doesn't awaken in that time," muttered Hackworth.

"She won't," interposed Williams quickly. "Only Terry's voice can bring her back."

Hackworth arose and gripped Grant's hand in silent gratitude…

* * * *

The next day Hackworth decided to show his cousin something of the internal workings of the modern New York.

"Dan," he said, "one of the reasons the standard of living is so high now is that machines do a great deal of the world's work. Unitaria, especially, is a highly specialized civilization. What has to be done is easily accomplished by a maximum working week of fifteen hours, and the total production is so great that there is more than enough for the comfort of all. I'll take you to see the machines in various industries."

Using electro-car transportation, they spent a whole day going around New York. Williams lost himself in wonder. Factories were large, clean establishments crammed with a bewildering maze of machines, guided by humans who looked puny and futile beside them. Tireless metallic moving parts twinkled up and down and in and out. Finished products spewed forth in steady streams into automatic receivers that carried them away for packing and distribution.

How efficient and quiet it all was! There was no suggestion of old-time sweaty, grimy, ill-ventilated, gloomy, screeching machine-rooms.

Their final stop was at the food products Branch E, where Terry worked. The Unidum had long ago taken over all food products, so important to humanity. Branch E produced only one thing—a vita-minized powder which went into all foods in Unitaria.

Terry took them through the plant. He brought them first before a series of seven apparatuses that seemed to be a hybrid between an enlarged clockwork and a chemical laboratory. Pumps drove colored liquids through thick quartz tubes; misted gases swirled violently in transparent chambers; huge rollers ground in flat pans containing heaps of lumped materials.

"These seven machines," exclaimed Terry, "are the initial steps in the manufacture of the seven vitamins needed in a balanced diet. Into them the raw products are fed through those chutes, starting the build-ing of the intricate vitamin molecules. Before the new compounds undergo further chemical reaction, they are tested by analysts."

The next room also housed seven machines, but vastly different. These were a conglomerate of millions of tubes, retorts, boiling liq-uids, and swirling solutions.

"Here," said Terry, "the molecules are further rearranged toward the ultimate vitamin molecules. Rigid tests are performed. Batches now and then have to be thrown out."

In each room were new and strange apparatuses. Hundreds tended them and took out samples for testing. Yet, strangely enough, no one actually seemed to have anything to do with the machinery. In the other industries there had always been men before control-boards. Here the machines went on endlessly as though having been once started, there could be no fluctuation in their production.

"These machines are marvelous," Williams remarked. "Are they built so perfectly that no interference with them is necessary?"

"They used to have control-boards," answered Terry, "but five years ago this plant was outfitted with a controlling mechanism that replaced human attendance. Only when a part wears out or breaks down, must a human being use his hands."

"What sort of control mechanism can that be?"

"I'll show you."

But Hackworth made them pause.

"Let's pass that up," he said in an oddly hurried voice. "It's—er—look how late it is. We must get home for dinner."

"Dinner can wait!" cried Williams, and he turned to Terry, but the chemist seemed perturbed. A covert look passed between him and Hackworth.

"Perhaps you'd rather—go home to dinner," said Terry.

Williams looked from one to the other. "Well, what is it?" he asked quietly.

Terry looked helplessly at Hackworth.

"I'm sorry. I should have thought—"

"Never mind, Terry," Hackworth said. "We could not have withheld it indefinitely, anyway. Dan, the controlling mechanism for all these machines is—*a brain. A human brain!"*

Williams almost staggered.

"*Sarto je Bru!*" he gasped. "A *living brain?*"

"No!" Hackworth said rapidly. "Not in the true sense of the word, but—" He broke off and began again. "A brain taken from a dead body and rejuvenated so that it can still perform mental tasks. Technically, I don't suppose anybody can explain how it's done, except the Scientists."

"The Scientists again!" burst out Williams. "It sounds as inhuman as the Eugenics Law." He breathed deeply as though controlling violent emotions. "Let's go and see it," he said quietly.

Terry led the way to the floor above where rooms contained stores of chemicals. In the exact center of the building was a circular chamber from which came the sound of clicking.

They stepped in and onto a platform surrounded by a railing. A neon sign above read:

VISITORS MUST NOT SMOKE

The sight that met Williams' eyes brought an involuntary cry to his lips. The entire wall-surface, with the exception of the part near the doorway, was taken up by an unbroken control-board with thousands of relays—tiny contact magnets, and pilot lights. There was a constant ticking and twinkling of the tiny globes. Across the ceiling stretched innumerable wires to the affair in the center of the room.

This object riveted Williams' gaze. It consisted of a cylindrical solid base of metal surmounted by an intricate system of mirrors and tubes. But topping that was another object that brought a quick contraction to Williams' brow—a circular glass globe suspended from the ceiling by a thick rod of metal. From it led thousands of fine silver wires, which connected to the mirrored mechanism below. From the globe two thin tubes ran parallel to a black metal box on the floor.

"The brain!" murmured Williams.

He could faintly make out the irregular outline of a grayish object suspended in a viscid liquid in the globe.

Terry began softly explaining, for Williams would ask about it.

"The brain is suspended in a nutritive fluid which is pumped up and down those two tubes from the black box that contains what might be called a mechanical heart. The mirrors and photo-electric tubes are the 'eyes' of the brain, with which it examines the readings of the gauges next to the wall relays. By some intricate system of semi-nerve control, it operates the various relays and switches which keep the machines below running smoothly and regularly."

"How can one brain control so many machines, when it would take dozens of attendants otherwise?"

"Because every cell of the brain is used. In life we never use the full capacity of our brains. Much of it lies dormant, subconscious."

"Surely the brain can't do anything if a part breaks down?"

"No. The brain merely controls the power input and product output, and takes care of variations. If the raw product put into any one machine happens to be especially hard to grind into powder, the Brain-control automatically adjusts the timing. But whenever repairs are needed, the Brain-control merely flashes a signal to the central office where the official in charge sends a repairman. Sometimes for days all the machines operate without human hands, except for routine testing."

Dan Williams, suddenly sickened, turned away. They all went to the Hackworth home for dinner, all feeling depressed and subdued. Afterward they smoked and talked desultory fashion, but Williams avoided all reference to the Brain-control.

Then Hackworth turned deathly white, for Williams had just asked a question Hackworth had hoped he never would.

"Where was my sister Helen buried?"

Seeing his cousin's face in a flash, Williams' eyes bored into Hackworth's, and Earl Hackworth knew those steady blue eyes would detect the slightest sign of prevarication. "Don't—*don't* ask me that!"

"I want to know," said Williams implacably. "The truth."

Hackworth waved a hand that said, "Then I have no choice." And in a choked voice he said aloud: "Helen's body was cremated by the Unidum, after her brain was removed and—"

"Helen's brain!" cried Williams, his face working.

He trailed off into muttered Bantu dialect. Hackworth sat there in misery. He had prayed that this need never come to light, but had known it was inevitable.

He waited for his bronzed cousin to break out in violent anger, but when Williams spoke, his voice was quiet, ominously controlled.

# CHAPTER VI

Nodding, as he caught a sign from Hackworth, Terry began to speak, for he was more familiar with the scientific aspects of the modern world than the explorer.

"Just five years ago, Mr. Williams," the young chemist explained, "a Scientist whose name is unknown succeeded in an experiment upon which he had been working for years. He announced that it was possible to take the brain from a person immediately after death, and bring back to it a semblance of life, a semi-subconscious existence. This rejuvenated brain could exert its full intellectual resources, if given a mechanical contact with the living world.

"Immediately the Scientists saw a use for such a dead-alive brain—a substitute for a group of living brains. The Unidum decided to use them for the benefit of the state."

"Why?" asked Williams. "Already working hours are short. If the Brain-control can take the place of fifty workers, it means little."

Terry nodded. "But suppose *all* machines were given Brain-control! That would release millions of workers, cut the working week still farther."

"And everybody would die of boredom," Williams snorted. "Earl tells me the people of Unitaria hardly know what to do with their leisure time now. What possible advantage would *more* leisure be?"

Terry shook his head. "The Unidum has been rather secretive about motives. At present there are only about two thousand Brain-controls in Unitaria, and the only machines fitted with them are the food products systems. But I've heard, confidentially, that the Unidum is determined to increase the use of them."

"But why?" repeated Williams, and he quoted, "'Idle hands do mischief make.'"

"Dan," said Hackworth defiantly, "the Unidum has ruled wisely for years, always with an eye to the future. They *must* have plans to balance the shifting amounts of work and leisure."

Williams sprang to his feet and strode up and down the room. "Somehow," he muttered, "there seems to be something sinister behind it. Can the Unidum be retrograding, as all systems of government in history have done after reaching a peak?" Hackworth and Terry shot guarded glances at one another. Dan Williams was putting into words things that were not breathed in Unitaria.

"And what is the public attitude toward the Brain-controls?" demanded Williams. "If the public dares to have an attitude in this day of scientific dictatorship."

"The workers who guide machines," Hackworth told him, "see a day when everyone will be his own master. But to tell the truth, there has been much disapproval from those who believe it is sacrilegious to—to disturb the dead, as you also believe."

"And as *you* do!" said Williams quickly.

"Yes, as I do," admitted Hackworth soberly.

"Terry," said Williams, facing the chemist, "what more can you tell me about the brain that is used like a piece of supersensitive machinery? To control machinery it must *think*, and if it thinks it is not really *dead*, and it must have emotion or consciousness."

Hackworth remonstrated, but Terry answered the demand in Williams' eyes.

"Yes, they *do* feel!" he cried, and faced the father of the girl he loved despairingly. "Mr. Hackworth, there's no use holding anything back. Nothing can be denied. I'll tell him all!"

Hackworth slumped back in his chair.

"The brains do feel!" repeated Terry, his eyes on Williams. "Enough to make it purgatory for them! *They* know, and *they* live in an endless torment! I'm constantly tortured by the thought of that sentient brain upstairs, sending impulses through cold silver wires, directing dozens of complicated machines. It cannot rebel! But it can remember life, can know pain, weariness, despair, futile anger. Two Scientists investigated and proved it. They were not blinded by scientific zeal, but when they attempted to tell the world, the Unidum hounded them, drove them out, perhaps killed them—no one knows. What they had learned leaked out, but only a few, like myself, believe them. The rest are content to think of the Brain-controls as organic machinery, and to believe the Unidum which promises a time when everybody will work only a few hours. They forget the misery of the brains! They forget that for everyone there can be no more 'Rest in Peace' now!"

Hackworth was astonished at Terry's outburst, but Williams' reaction was fearful to see. Livid fire shot from his eyes. His lips twisted. Zulus had seen that expression and turned ashen under their black skin. It was a compound of mighty rage and purple hatred. Terry shivered as he saw powerful shoulders knot into corded muscles under the man's shirt.

Suddenly Williams relaxed. He glanced at the other two men apologetically. "Earl," he asked, "how did they come to use Helen's— brain?"

"It was just at the time the first Brain-controls were made that Helen died. The brains of those who died on a certain day were conscripted by the Unidum. They were 'honored' in being the first to initiate that 'great advancement in science.' There were riots that day— friends and relatives of the 'honored' deceased. But the Unidum did not see then that it had made its greatest mistake in authorizing the use of Brain-controls. It does not see it now, nor care to see it."

"Has there been no organized opposition?"

"Not as yet, although feeling has run high at times."

"*Sarto!*" exclaimed Williams. "An inhuman horror like that and nothing is done! And the Eugenics Law, also inhuman, and there are no people of spirit to revolt."

"Revolt? The Unidum is all-powerful—practically a dictatorship. And to the Scientists the Eugenics Law and the Brain-control are laudable advancements. What can you expect the masses to do when the Unidum has given them benefits never known on Earth before? I've told you, Dan, the Unidum has done far more good than harm."

"The mere thought of Helen—" said Williams. "Where is the Brain-control which—"

"I don't know."

"You do!"

Hackworth sweated under the adamant demand of his cousin, then whispered: "Boston."

"Then I'm going to Boston! If it's the last act of my life, I'm going to see that my sister's brain dies its proper death!"

"You're mad!"

"Do you think I could live in peace, or die in peace, knowing that all that is still conscious of Helen, lies in perpetual torment?"

"But there is nothing you can do! It's been tried before." Hackworth turned with pleading to the young chemist. "You tell him, Terry!"

"That's right, Mr. Williams," said Terry. "You could do nothing."

"I can wreck the whole control."

"Even if you break all the contacts and smash the mirror-eyes," returned Terry, "the brain does not die. As long as the nutritive fluid surrounds it, it lives. You can't harm that because the mechanical heart is enclosed in heavy steel. No key will open its lock except the one in the hands of the Scientist who renews the fluid periodically. The pipes leading upward are out of reach. So is the brain-case out of reach."

"What would a well-aimed bullet do if it struck the brain-case?"

"Why, smash it. But you need a gun for that."

"And you can't get a gun no matter how hard you try," interposed Hackworth. "Remember I left all my guns at Kabinda? No one can import a gun into Unitaria. And none are sold here. The Unidum has completely disarmed the citizens of Unitaria."

Williams drew his brows together thoughtfully. "Nevertheless," he said grimly, "I'm going to Boston. Somehow I'll figure out a way."

"But Lila! Dan, you haven't forgotten—"

"No, Earl. However, we can do nothing until we hear from Andrew Grant. I'll go to Boston and—"

"You'll do nothing rash?" pleaded Hackworth. "The Unidum is quick to punish, and Lila might be involved through you."

But abruptly Williams said good night and left the room.

Hackworth turned a grave face to young Spath. "There was a close bond between Dan and his sister. Perhaps it would be wise for you, Terry, to go to Boston with him."

"Certainly," agreed the young chemist. "I can get the day off."

"I'm going to keep M'bopo here. In his present mood, Dan is liable to get violent. If M'bopo is along, one word in dialect will start him fighting, and the two of them could make plenty of trouble. Perhaps after Dan realizes his helplessness, he will gradually calm down…"

In his room, Williams carefully unwrapped the layers of hide in the soft light of a shaded lamp and looked at the contents of his bundle. There was a tiger's tooth of odd shape, reputed to be a potent charm, other trinkets with a history, and a soft giraffe skin pouch which he intended as a gift for Lila. He put the tiger's tooth in his pocket with a sheepish grin. Africa had left in him a vestige of native superstition.

He fingered the other articles, talking about them to M'bopo, then heaped them on the dresser-top.

Undressing, he looked through the window at suburban New York. It had started raining, a warm September rain. It blurred the scenery until he saw a sweeping jungle, a shadowed desert, gnus grazing in the brush.

He started. No, this was not Africa; it was Unitaria. It was a world with hyp-marines, Sansrun aircraft, spanned cities, a new government, and a multitude of blessings to mankind. But then there was the Eugenics Law—and the Brain-control.

Even in his sleep, with M'bopo stretched out on the rug beside his bed, he clenched his fists. . . .

As the giant six-motored passenger plane hurtled high above New York on its way to Boston, Williams took a last look at the city below. Like a geometrician's paradise it spread back from the ocean, bizarrely unreal in the gloom of a cloudy day. He could faintly make out the Unidum capitol, then the city faded into murkiness. Below was farmland, ribboned with broad highways along which tiny dots moved incessantly.

Williams was in a blank mood. The revelations of the evening before had seemed grotesque after a night's sleep. Brains in machines! How impossible. Brains, officially dead, with an after-life! Running machinery. Thinking, sending out nervous impulses—*feeling*!

*Sarto*! Could such a thing be? Was Terry wrong? Could the consciousness that had once been Helen Williams be captured in a glass globe and forced to do endless relay-manipulations? Could the brain of that girl be in a state where the memories of life tortured it while some influence kept its nerve centers throbbing messages along silver wires?

Williams turned to Terry who was beside him. He must clear his mind of whirling conjecture.

"While we have the chance, Terry," he said, "suppose you tell me something more about this age in which we live. I know only too little of it as yet. Tell me about motive power, what fuels and energies you use, anything else of interest."

Terry willingly launched into the subject, glad that Williams no longer was brooding.

"In the year when you left America on your African exploration," he said, "coal and natural oil furnished the bulk of power in Europe and America. Today, forty years later, half of Unitaria's power output is from a dream of your own time come true—tide-machines. After World War Two it had been thought that at once atomic energy would be converted to commercial use, but that is still a hope and a dream. The sea-coast cities, and those a few hundred miles inland, are supplied with cheap electrical power. Up and down every important coast are large tide-stations, which convert the tide movements into hundreds of thousands of kilowatts of energy. From these it is wired via beryllium cables to the various cities. Much of this power is then transmitted for use through ether broadcast.

"In New York the electro-cars are run without overhead trolleys or third rails. They get their power from the ether. I won't attempt to describe—I couldn't—the complex system of automatic units which attach beams of radio energy between the central power station and the great numbers of electrocars. Inland cities as far west as Pittsburgh are supplied with ether energy from the Long Island tide-stations.

"No more coal then, no miner's strikes?" asked Williams.

"No strikes," Terry grinned. "But there's coal. The other half of Unitaria's power still comes from natural deposits of coal and oil. But oil is petering out and supplies but a small part. Today coal is never burned as such. The gases and tars are extracted for the chemical industries, just as they were forty years ago, and only the coke is used for power. Yet neither is the coke burned! By what is called 'hydrogenation' it is converted into oils and gasolines, which burn much more efficiently than the coke.

"This liquid fuel runs railroad trains, aircraft, automobiles, and ocean craft. All Diesel engines burn coke-oil. In cities so far inland that it is impossible to make use of tide-power, internal combustion engines make electricity which is used directly, without ether broadcast. In central Europe, in what used to be Germany, rocket-turbines are being used with fair success. Places that produce water power are still in operation, as Niagara, and a certain amount of wind power is also produced.

"With the advent of cheap oil from coal, aircraft immediately began replacing surface transportation methods, and that replacing process is still going on. Perhaps in another forty years, everything will go through the air. Hyp-marines which carry half the ocean commerce are really aircraft more than anything else."

"And so I take it," Williams commented soberly, "that just as men in nineteen thirty-three dreamed of tide-engines and rocket motive power and stratosphere flights—now an accomplished fact—so do inventors today dream and labor toward atomic power and sun power engines, Earth-heat motors, and even gravity-nullifying apparatus. Probably, the next forty years will see those things too!"

# CHAPTER VII

Boston, revealed dimly in fog wisps, appeared to be a smaller edition of New York City. Spider spans and threads knitted its business section so heavily that Williams abstractedly wondered if all the buildings would rise if a Cyclops were to pick up one with a suitably large tweezers. Like an artificial whale, a hyp-marine was coming over the horizon, skimming the water.

Their ship began to descend, then it bored to a position over the tall buildings and swooped gently. It landed like an angry dragon on the immense flat roof of the main air terminal.

"Do you know which Brain-control we want to see?" asked Williams as he and Terry walked away from the ship along the pedestrian path.

"There is only one in Boston," said Terry, "as in all large cities except New York and London, which have two each. As yet the use of Brain-controls is little better than experimental."

"An experiment that should never have been tried," muttered Williams.

Escalators took them to one of the hanging platform stations of the public transportation systems. Looking at the electro-car that slid to a noiseless stop, Williams found it hard to believe that it derived its power from an ether beam.

Ten minutes of blurring speed brought them to Branch G of Boston food products, similar to Branch E in New York, except that the all-important Brain-control was on the ground floor.

Williams approached the Brain-control room with a thumping heart. They entered, and slowly, fearfully, he turned his eyes to the luminescent globe suspended from the ceiling.

"*Je Bru il Bra!*" Sweat broke on his forehead and he pulled his gaze away, unable to look at the globe that held his sister's brain.

As he dropped his eyes, he saw a man standing before the black box at the base of the cylindrical mirror support. Dark-haired and burly, in conventional clothing with a light blue cape over his shoulders, he was busy at the black box.

"A Scientist!" whispered Terry. "Changing the nutritive supply."

Here was the first of that group of 1973 "Scientists" that Williams had seen. On the back of the man's cape was a design of a robot and girl, with a background of intricate machinery under the sun and blue sky. The fellow, in the prime of life, worked with sure fingers, his back turned to block a view of the box, the heavy steel door of which was open. But they saw him move a tall glass jar filled with a thick, colorless fluid and replace it with a similar jar after he connected the new jar with the pumping system.

Williams' eyes fastened to the globe. There was his sister's brain! That man, that Scientist, was putting in the mechanical heart a jar of liquid food that would give semi-life to—to Helen! So that she could continue to be a slave to the machines, could send continual nerve-impulses along cold silver wires. And all the while her consciousness, or whatever was imprisoned.

"Helen—Helen!" he called in his heart.

Perhaps she saw him standing there, might even now be pleading to him to release her from such horrible bondage.

She *was*! He could feel it—waves of subtle influence that shook his brain as an ultra-sound organ note shakes the ground.

Terry kept an anxious eye on Williams. He had seen the strong play of emotion in his face, in his fiery eyes, in the way he leaned against the rail. But what happened next, Terry was powerless to prevent.

With a hoarse shout, Williams vaulted over the rail, landed six feet below, catlike. Terry shouted, but it was too late. Mouthing shrill, primitive Bantu maledictions, Williams streaked toward the black box, powerful hands outstretched.

The Scientist whirled, and instantly banged shut the black box. But one ponderous swing from the arm of a brawny man lunging at him bowled him violently against the relays, unconscious.

Terry leaped to the floor, darted to Williams and attempted to bring him to reason. Williams brushed him away with a steel-spring arm and continued battering at the locked door of the black box. Only one thought burned in his brain—to smash the mechanical heart inside. But even his great muscles could not affect inch-thick metal.

Terry staggered erect, looked at the panting, cursing man who was tearing at the heavy pump-tubes above the box.

"We've got to get out of here!" Terry shouted, but knew Williams did not hear.

A red light was flashing intermittently. The alarm signal!

"The guards—they will be here any moment!"

Williams must have realized its significance, for he suddenly ceased his futile battering and looked around desperately. His eye caught sight of a small wrench the Scientist had used to fit the couplings on the necks of the jars.

With a savage cry of triumph, Williams picked it up and hurled it at the brain-globe. It glanced off the glass without breaking it!

In the midst of a shattering sound of fragile mirrors and photo-electric tubes, came the shouts of men crowding the platform. Men in uniforms of blue and red and shiny leather swarmed toward them— Unidum police.

Terry fought side by side with Williams, with bare fists. Why, he did not know, except that some breath of battle had flowed from the man at his side to activate him. Williams was a human cyclone, powered by Herculean muscles which plunged piston-like at sweating, grunting guards who could lay no hand on him.

In sudden exaltation, Terry threw his full strength into the battle. It was a sensation new to him, pounding at faces. It was exhilarating. He forgot everything except that he and Williams were beset by enemies who must be knocked off their feet. The savage pleasure of it dimmed his reason. Neither he nor Williams saw the man stealthily creeping back of them, with a pistol-like object in his hand.

It was suddenly over. The two embattled men staggered and crumpled to the floor, paralyzed by an electric shock.

\* \* \* \*

That evening, in the prison section of the Boston Science Court, they were waiting for the trial which would be given them immediately.

"I'm sorry, and in a way not sorry," said Williams through swollen lips. "I'm sorry I got you into a mess, Terry. But I'm *not* sorry that I tried my level best to smash that globe."

"I understand," Terry said. "I would have been driven to knock over Professor Jorgen, the Scientist who wants to marry Lila, had I ever met him."

"Justice moves swiftly in nineteen seventy-three," said Williams.

"Yes, especially when the charge is treason against the Unidum!"

"Treason?" repeated Williams.

Terry nodded glumly. "The Brain-control is Unidum property. They will charge us with being connected with some secret organization plotting against the Unidum. The jury will be composed of Scientists. Their verdict will be unalterable and the sentence"—Terry shuddered—"more than we deserve."

"Would it help to tell the truth? About Helen?"

"I'm sure it wouldn't," Terry said. "Williams, I'm willing to plead guilty to treasonable action against the Unidum. This will cut short the trial and prevent the implication of Hackworth—and perhaps Lila."

"I will, also," said Williams. "Only I wish you had never come with me."

Williams cursed himself. Why had he ever done such a thing so futile and thoughtless there in the Brain-control room? He had lost his head completely. He had metamorphosed into a savage jungle creature. *Sarto*! He had actually imagined that his sister's brain had entreated him to give her soul freedom! It had swept all sane thought from his mind.

Immersed in gloom and feeling the throbs of bruises and wrenched muscles, they spoke little.

The trial was short that evening. It took place in a huge courtroom filled with curious crowds. The judge, emotionless and stern, peered at the defendants as though they were irresponsible children. Every man of the jury wore the blue cape with the symbolic insignia of Science. The atmosphere of the place was cold, implacable, pitiless. Facing the jury of Scientists, Terry and Williams pleaded guilty to treasonable action against the Unidum. This prevented the Scientists from putting in any further charge of conspiracy.

The sentence—what would that be? Williams looked at the austere frown on the judge's brow and knew it could not be light. Terry's face was bloodless and drawn.

Then came the sentence. The words struck Williams like powerful blows.

"—just punishment will be painless death by gas, with the unmerited honor of having their cerebral organs installed in Brain-controls in the—"

There was deathly silence. Terry, beside Williams, had turned to stone.

Death? Could that be their *sentence*?

Everyone in the courtroom, even the Scientists, shuddered at the sudden harsh laugh that came from the older of the two men. Then he was led away. But at the door he jerked to a stop and faced the quiet courtroom. His voice rang out:

"Some day the Unidum will be sorry it ever permitted the inhuman Brain-control to become lawful!"

There were murmurs from the crowd and the Scientists looked at one another uneasily. The judge reddened in anger and waved for the prisoners to be taken out.

Escorted by a dozen Unidum guards, they were taken to a different cell. The door clanged shut, the key grated and there was silence. On Williams' face was a queer look of defiance, but his eyes were dazed; the dread sentence had struck hard.

"*My* brain in a Brain-control! What diabolical irony! If I had only succeeded in releasing Helen, then it would be easier to take. Terry, for ages the memory of having failed in that will run through my dead-alive brain!" He went on vehemently. "But they haven't executed us yet, and may the Seven Devils of the Seven Hills of Ok-Ok eat my heart out if I lose hope of escape!"

Terry thought the man had gone mad, for he began to prowl about the dark cell as though looking for a secret doorway. He stopped at the real door and shook its heavy bars experimentally. Nothing could be solider. The cell was steel-lined. On the window were heavy steel bars like those on the door.

Through it could be seen the fairy-like picture of Boston at night, but it was impossible to see the street level sixty stories down. The dark bulk of a huge enclosed span jutted from the building, extending across the street canyon. It carried electro-car service to the Unidum Sub-headquarters.

Terry sat down with a feeling of pity for the older man. Apparently the strain had unsettled his mind. Perhaps he thought he was back in Africa, imprisoned in some rickety thatch hut he could batter down if he wished. Certainly from his twitching lips came a muttered stream of clipped African gibberish.

That there was no escape, Terry knew. There were hundreds of Unidum police throughout the building. The door's lock could not be picked for it had no keyhole on the inside. The walls were proof against human strength. And the one and only window let out upon a sheer drop of a thousand feet.

When the crouching Williams sneaked to the window and cocked one ear as though hearing something besides the drone of aircraft above, Terry thought it time to do something. Gently, but firmly, he tugged him away from the window, and pushed him to the wall bunk. Williams struggled, then fell back flat. He slept.

Terry threw himself on his own bunk.

# CHAPTER VIII

For hours after Terry and Williams had left for Boston Hackworth spent his time writing of his trip to interior Congo, a comprehensive report which he planned sending to the Federated States of Africa. M'bopo displayed a degree of intelligence in aiding him that surprised Hackworth as the Bantu traced unerringly the ramifications of the route along unexplored rivers and through unnamed deserts.

When Terry and Williams failed to appear for dinner he began to worry. Yet what could have happened, with Terry along? Probably taking in a few of the sights around Boston.

At seven o'clock Hackworth tuned in the radio news, still uneasy. His worst suspicions were confirmed as the announcer told of the hectic fight in the Brain-control room and that Williams and Spath, finally subdued and jailed, were to be sentenced by the Science Court.

Hackworth cursed his cousin, cursed Terry, and reviled the Unidum. When M'bopo stuck his head in the doorway, and he poured out the trouble to him in a mixture of Bantu and English, M'bopo stood as though frozen.

"Let us go," said M'bopo. "I will fight. *Sarto Bru*! I will kill all the guards and take *Orno Akku* from prison."

"No, no!" said Hackworth. "This is not Africa, M'bopo. There are hundreds of guards. They will kill *you*."

"I do not care," replied the other impassively. "Take me to *Orno Akku*."

Hackworth suddenly realized that M'bopo was not asking, but demanding.

"All right, M'bopo. But not tonight. They would not let us in. Tomorrow morning we will go."

M'bopo grunted and sat down cross-legged on the floor.

The next morning Hackworth and M'bopo were in the foyer of the Unidum Sub-headquarters in Boston. At nine o'clock they were led to the sixtieth story.

The two prisoners were dejectedly standing at the window. They turned in surprise when the door swung open.

"Hackworth!" cried Terry. "I suppose this was on the radio?"

"Last night," answered Hackworth. "Dan—"

"I know," interrupted Williams. "How could I be such a fool? I can hardly explain it myself. As I stood there looking at the globe and realized that Helen's brain was in it, something snapped."

Hackworth nodded. "You're hardly to be blamed."

"And now," said Williams bitterly, "our brains are to be used in Brain-controls!"

Hackworth had not heard that. He gasped, and his eyes reflected a great horror. He knew, only too well, that the execution would take place in three days. All sentences for treasonable crimes were consummated or started in three days.

"Lila! Lila!" moaned Hackworth. "What will happen to her? With Terry gone she will never wake up again!"

"Yes she will," assured Williams. "Eventually the drug will lose its effect. But she will awaken only to find Terry gone and a Scientist husband awaiting her."

The three men looked at one another. Everything had now gone awry, for there would be no purpose in freeing Lila from the Eugenics Law with Terry dead.

"We *must* try to do something!" said Hackworth suddenly, pacing up and down. "Jail-breaking is impossible—"

Hackworth's voice sank to a whisper. "Perhaps I can bribe the man with the keys. Or I might approach higher authority and let the sunlight flash on gold. I've got less than three days... I'll do what I can."

Terry and Williams smiled wanly. By now even Williams had seen clearly how impossible it was to flee their prison.

But his tones were not confident, and Terry gave no sign of interest. They knew the Unidum.

M'bopo suddenly confronted Williams.

"*Orno Akku* wishes to go free?" he asked in Bantu.

"M'bopo will fight for you. We will kill the guards and fly away in a metal bird."

"No, M'bopo," said Williams. "There are too many guards; they have guns, and a clever alarm system."

"Then I will stay here with you."

It took Williams minutes to convince M'bopo that his loyalty was misplaced. Then the guard at the door announced that their time was up and Hackworth and M'bopo were forced to leave.

The public landing field and hangar where Hackworth had left his Sansrun was on top of a building a block away. As they entered the plane and it took altitude, they passed several rows of windows heavily barred in the Unidum building.

"*Orno Akku* is in one of them," said Hackworth, indicating the windows.

M'bopo suddenly recognized William's face peering out of one of them. He pointed it out excitedly and Hackworth swung as close as the lane signals would allow to wave good-by.

He felt a clutch on his arm. Words poured into his ear—Bantu words, startling words. Hackworth listened, asked a few questions. The replies brought a thoughtful gleam to his eyes.

He guided his Sansrun along turns that circled the Unidum Sub-headquarters and climbed across the barred windows which framed Williams' tanned face. Then Hackworth, absorbed in the consideration of certain configurations, sent the ship away from Boston. All the way back to New York, he and M'bopo talked excitedly. Could it be done? It was worth a trial…

That night, lying on his bunk in a darkness broken only by the dim light that came through the window, Williams found it hard to sleep. Terry's regular breathing came to him except when the drone of an airplane filled the little cell.

Williams asked himself, tossing fitfully, whether there was any hope. No. Hackworth could do nothing, even with his entire wealth. Andrew Grant could do nothing. And there was no one else to help; they were doomed. First the death, then awakening of some mystic sort with the gradual realization of being a part of a complicated apparatus forced to send nerve-impulses along thin silver wires! Already Williams seemed to hear the clicking of magnet relays. He had to keep repeating to himself that he was not a Brain-control yet. But the clicking! It was still there! And a sibilant sound—like rubbing!

He jerked up his head. The sound came from the window. There was something there! He leaped from the bunk toward the window—and stumbled over a rope! A small stone at one end of it was clicking as the rope was dragged slowly across the floor by its other end.

Williams did not stop to ponder, but quickly tied the rope to a bar, giving it a jerk to indicate its being done. After scraping sounds outside, M'bopo appeared, panting. One of his hands gripped a bar; then the other. M'bopo's wiry arm muscles pulled his body upward till his knees rested on the window ledge.

"M'bopo! What is this?"

"*Orno Akku*! I come to rescue you. The way I come, that way you go."

"How did you come?"

"I climb down long box that crosses ditch. I balance rope. I walk to end of rope. I jump. Here I am." In a flash Williams understood, though M'bopo's Bantu could barely cover the subject. "Long box" was the nearby electro-car enclosed span. "Rope" was cable support.

"But these bars, M'bopo!" Williams said excitedly. The other probed in his pockets and brought out a small bottle which he handed through the bars.

"You hurry, *Orno Akku*. Hackworth, he waits."

And Williams did hurry, but not with nervous rapidity. He had suddenly become calm, efficient with a cold haste. A hand on Terry's shoulder, a few whispered words, and the young chemist became imbued with the same swift efficiency. Their lives depended on how quickly they worked.

Williams crouched near the door, his ear against it. Terry opened the bottle, poured some of its contents at the base of one of the window bars. There was a prolonged hiss. Then the bar was loose, completely eaten through. Another drawn-out hiss and again a bar was loose. Five bars were treated. Terry thanked the gods that an acid existed which attacked steel as viciously and quickly as sodium metal attacks water.

Williams knew there had never been a compound like that in 1933. When the final bar had been eaten away by the acid, he leaped to the window, grasped the first bar and pulled. Terry held M'bopo by the belt as the steel gave and curled upward. With a frantic strength, they bent the other four.

"Now," said Williams, panting, "comes the hardest part. That cable support that leads to the span is about ten feet below, says M'bopo. We must climb down the rope to the cable, then walk along it to the span. And"—he looked steadily at Terry—"it's a thousand feet straight down."

"Let's go," Terry said steadily.

Williams motioned for him to go first and Terry lost no time in clambering through the window. His first glance at the view from his precarious perch on the sill brought a chill to his heart. Far below, only partially revealed by lights, was the ground level. At various heights were both enclosed and platform spans, hung with red lights. All about were the cadaverous heights of slim towers. It was a dizzying spectacle. Terry recovered his shaken nerves, twisted carefully about, and lowered himself, glad to feel the firm rope in his hands. He descended hand over hand until his feet struck something solid, and a strong hand steadied him. M'bopo's round eyes peered into his.

In another moment, Williams came down the rope and all three of them stood crowded on the flat cable-lug joined to the building. A cool autumn breeze whistled around the wall and quickly took the perspiration off their brows.

"All right," whispered Williams. "I listened at the door just before I left through the window. Apparently none of the guards have heard a sound. But the longer we hesitate, the more chance we take. M'bopo, *umo ulka dis*. He'll go first, Terry. Then you. Do you think you can manage without help?"

Terry watched the Bantu, without answering. The cable support for the nearby span stretched taut, enclosing a triangle with the building and the span housing. It was a hundred feet long and M'bopo, arms outstretched and slightly crouched to balance the gentle breeze, negotiated the cable without pause, as sure-footed as a mountain goat. His body gradually faded into the gloom at the side of the span.

"I could hold your hand," suggested Williams, "or your belt."

Suddenly realizing that he must seem craven in the older man's eyes, for not having answered his question, Terry looked into his eyes.

"I go alone, Williams. If I fall, there is no need for you to fall *with* me."

Williams gripped his hand encouragingly. It was one thing for M'bopo and himself, long trained in Africa in physical pursuits, to traverse the cable, but quite another for a man reared in civilization. Such a man does not have the fine balance and muscular coordination of a child of nature.

Nevertheless, Terry stepped away from the cable-lug with set jaw, determined to do or die. He took the first ten steps confidently and began to feel that his first fears were silly. But at the next step, a gust of wind pushed at him. Off-balance, he blindly put his free foot forward and only by sheerest luck touched the cable with his toe. Back of him a voice called encouragement. It was no time to hesitate and recover breath or nerve, so Terry plunged recklessly forward, barely able to see the cable at his feet.

He steeled himself not to look past the support, knowing that one glance at the pit under him would paralyze every muscle in his body. Breathing hard, swaying, and moving steadily forward, Terry forgot everything but the cable, his feet, and the wind. It seemed hours on end that he alternately lifted his feet and set them down. He dared not look up nor to the side.

He wondered how far he was. Was this an eternal nightmare? Already he had tramped miles. His leg muscles ached as though he had run a marathon. He was getting dizzy. The constant stare of concentration at the cable was bringing spots to his eyes. He was swaying! The wind, in spiteful little gusts, would—

Terry felt his front foot barely scrape the cable. It slipped and he knew it was over. Suddenly limp and hopeless, he felt himself toppling—toppling into that deep pit between buildings. His body would drop like a stone, past five spans, down to the hard street. Nothing would stop it!

Now what had happened, wondered Terry. Something had grabbed his belt. Something strained at his body that was hanging over the pit with one foot only on the cable. And that something pulled him back from the abyss.

Terry's brain cleared. M'bopo was there with a hand in his belt, looking at him in mute inquiry. Terry waved forward, again on balance. One—two—three steps, and then Terry felt the welcome solidity of a broad, flat surface. They were on the span's roof! He had lost his balance and almost fallen only three steps from safety.

M'bopo was grinning, and large beads of sweat stood out on his brow. Only he would ever realize how much superhuman, agonizing strength it had taken to pull the falling white man upright, and at the constant risk of losing his own balance should the torque shift too suddenly from limp body to straining muscles.

There was a sound of running feet, then a familiar voice as a figure loomed up from farther along the roof of the span. "Terry, my boy! Thank God you made it!"

"Mr. Hackworth! But how did you—"

"Explanations later. Must get away as quickly as possible."

They turned to watch the dim figure coming along the cable. Without hesitation, firmly and swiftly, Williams moved along. There was an indefinable grace about him and a boyish elasticity that made it hard for Terry to realize how old a man he was in point of years. Certainly no younger man could have performed the feat any easier.

Williams came up with a rush, waving a jubilant arm. "All here safe and sound!" he exclaimed, nodding to Hackworth. "No delay now. Into the ship, all of us!"

As they ran toward the dark hull of Hackworth's Sansrun, they heard the rumble of an electro-car beneath them. Terry smiled, wondering what the passengers would think or say if they knew that on the roof under which they streaked were four jail-breakers and an outlaw ship. How simple—and wonderful—it had been, after all, when but an hour before escape had seemed absolutely impossible!

Williams closed the cabin door behind them. Hackworth was already at the controls. But before starting the motors, he had them all look around for a possible lurking police ship. It was against the law to land on a span; detection would bring immediate pursuit.

High above from the towers of the tallest buildings came the broad sweeps of aircraft beacons, ribboning the sky. Several of the important traffic lanes were bathed in constant light, revealing considerable night traffic. Where they were, beneath the lowest lane, it was a pocket of darkness between the lighted streets and the swinging searchlights.

Satisfied that no police ships were around, Hackworth brought the twin motors to life, idled them for a minute, then shot the ship upward. They climbed obliquely toward the neon-lighted spire of a lane mark, up and up out of the canyon of spans. Suddenly there were lane signals and Hackworth obediently leveled. He breathed a sigh of relief.

"The police danger is over. Now we're just one ship out of thousands."

He spoke too confidently, however. The pilot of a lumbering freighter, passing the Unidum Sub-headquarters to a landing a mile away, had seen the shadowed ship rise from the canyon. Suspicious as to the motives of a private ship coming from that forbidden direction, he reported the incident to the police after landing.

# CHAPTER IX

In the meantime, Hackworth piloted his ship away from Boston and headed in the gloom of the night to the south. He built up a fast but safe speed, high above the commercial lanes. Then he turned to his cousin. "Dan, you're a free man, at least for a while."

"Thanks to you, Earl."

"Thanks to M'bopo," corrected Hackworth. "It was his idea. At first I thought it hare-brained, then I saw how easy it would be to land the Sansrun on the span roof in the night. M'bopo claimed the rest would be just as easy."

Williams struck his head deprecatingly. "And to think it escaped me entirely! M'bopo, unlettered native as we call him, has scored against the all-powerful Unidum. It's a curious thought. Well"—he changed his tone—"the important thing is where do we go now?"

"You and Terry at present are outlaws," Hackworth said. "There will be a price on your heads. A peaceful life in Unitaria is impossible. You've got to get away to some place not governed by the Unidum."

"Never!" said Terry vehemently.

"Let me finish, Terry," said Hackworth quietly. "My plan is to negotiate your escape from Unitaria, with Lila! And after I've had my money transferred to foreign accounts, I'll join you. We can all live happily in some sheltered corner of Earth, free of the Unidum."

Hackworth's eyes shone as he went on. "Right now I am taking you to the Long Island Tide-station. The superintendent is a close friend of mine. I've already spoken to him. A tide-station is the place for you two to hide because the police are least likely to look for you there. You lie low and I will charter a stratosphere ship and somehow get Lila from the hospital. Andrew Grant will help me. Then—"

An exclamation from Terry cut him off. "Look! A ship is after us!"

They peered through the rear-vision mirror. With ominous purposefulness, a long, slim tri-motored plane hung on their trail, rapidly gaining. It could not be chance that it was following them, for both ships were out of the regular lanes.

"A Unidum police ship," Hackworth said. "I can tell by its shape." Terry confirmed it.

"That stops us," Hackworth said wearily. "It's possible they merely wonder why we fly so high and fast, but if they make us land and question us, we're done for."

But Williams was not so willing to admit defeat. "How long before we reach the tide-station? What you've told me about them gives me an idea. Even if the police know we're there, we're not in a hopeless position.

"We can get there in about twenty minutes at top speed. But there's no use trying to out-fly them, Dan. Besides, they're armed. They'll disable us. In a few minutes there will be more police ships here—"

"And there's the Stop-and-Land signal!" burst in Terry.

From the pursuing ship had flashed a thin beam of crimson light, flooding the cabin.

"Stop-and-land, never!" cried Williams, grasping Hackworth by the arm. "It's dark! Turn off the cabin lights and drop. Maneuver around, throw 'em off the track! Why should we give up so tamely after we've broken out of jail?"

Terry firmly motioned Hackworth away from the controls. "*I'll* give them a run-around!"

Plunged in darkness, Terry shot the ship down. Leveling gradually, he swung in a huge arc that would take them away from the police ship. From that plane now shot brilliant beams of white light which probed through the darkness, searching for the vanishing prey.

Then Terry cursed. To one side appeared more beams of dancing light. Some of the rays almost touched them and only a quick drop prevented it.

"They've got the whole Boston Patrol after us!" gasped Hackworth. "They must know we broke jail. They'll hem us in—"

"Not if I can help it," muttered Terry.

Williams encouraged him and their ship became a plunging, weaving thing, trying to escape the inexorable beams from dozens of police ships. It looked like a dance of the fireflies. Every so often, the fleeing ship would flicker in the chance beam of a light and the police ships would converge like vultures.

"If I only had more speed!" groaned Terry. "I can't draw away. I can only dodge!"

"No good, Terry," Williams said quietly. "They're gradually cutting us off on all sides. Can you give them a run as far as the tide-station without getting in range of their weapons?"

"Possibly, if we rise at full power. As a helicopter, we're their equal because they only have two adaptable engines. We *might* get as far as the tide-station. But a lot of good that will do."

"Try it!" said Williams.

Terry jammed his foot on the throttle and swung the air-screws upward. The beams of the police ships fell below, then again followed as flicker after flicker revealed the outlaw ship rising. But before they gained sufficient altitude to head off the fleeing ship, Terry had swung level at full speed. He flew over a police ship from which came a sudden scarlet flash.

"Missed!" breathed Terry. "They won't get another chance for some time."

Ten minutes of shattering flight, with the police gaining rapidly, brought them within sight of the tide-station at the tip of Long Island. It was an incredible affair, alien to eyes of 1933. Long concrete appendages reached out to sea for miles, dimly visible in reflected light. They radiated from a comparatively small building, flat and unadorned. In the exact center of its circular flat roof was a small brightly lit bubble, the control room. All the enormous electrical energy produced by the tides at that point was wired to cities as far north as Boston, and to New York.

Williams also knew one important thing about the tide-station which offered a slim hope of their again escaping the Unidum. At his order, Terry shot the plane downward, and landed on the flat roof.

"No time to talk," said Williams hurriedly. "Earl, lead the way to your friend, the superintendent."

Even as the four of them raced across the roof toward a lighted alcove from which steps led downward, one of the police ships descended with roaring motors. At the foot of the stairs Joe Manners, the superintendent, met them.

"Hackworth!" he cried. "You've ruined me! I saw—the police—"

"We've ruined nothing yet!" cried Williams. "Listen to me…"

In terse sentences, he unfolded his plan. Manners nodded and led their way along a corridor and then up steps. They emerged in a small room with a hemispherical ceiling. In it was only a desk, a chair, and a panel of dials and switches. But it was the master control-room of the station; from below came the hum of the giant tide-generators.

Manners closed the door and locked it. He glanced at the dial readings, turned.

"The plan will work only if we properly strike fear into their hearts."

"But will there be any trouble for you afterward?" asked Hackworth.

"I think not. Little is known of the technicalities of a tide-station to the average person, even the police. I will be able to squirm out of it. Anyhow, I have good reasons for wishing to help you in this predicament. You see—"

A loud knocking at the door cut him off. He signaled caution.

"Open for the Unidum police!" came in loud tones.

"I—I can't!" shouted back Manners with well-stimulated fear in his voice. "I am in the hands of desperate men who—" He choked as though he had received dire threats.

From the other side of the door came a jumbled murmur. Then again a voice: "Two of those men are criminals, sentenced to death for treason. They broke prison in Boston!"

"Oh, oh, oh!" moaned Manners. "What shall I do?"

"Shut up!" shouted Williams with well-timed ferocity.

"Hey, you!" came from the minions of the law. "Surrender, or it will go hard with you."

"Never!" shouted back Williams. "If we have to die, we'll choose our death. Rather than let you execute us, we will wreck this tide-station and die in its ruins!"

Manners pulled a little switch which sent a crackling spark across two fuse electrodes, then shouted in alarm, stamping his feet on the floor.

"Don't touch that switch!" he cried desperately.

The police, hearing the noises of a scuffle which sounded ominous, threw their weight against the door in an attempt to batter it down. But the door held.

"You'll blow up—"

"Get out of my way!"

"*Help*!"

"No help for you! Nor for the police! Nor for anybody!"

The words, the hoarse shouts, the scuffling noises, had their desired effect upon the police. The desperadoes in the control room were tampering with electrical dynamite, thousands of Kilowatts of it!

Then came Manners' voice again in a piercing scream. "The master switch! He pulled it! Let me out of here! The whole station will blow up! Fools, you've got just ten seconds to live! The blow-up starts right here."

The police stamped away from the door. When the noise of their running feet died away, the men in the little control room grinned at one another.

"It worked." Manners chuckled. Then he became serious. "Now's your chance! Fly away in the dark. I'll turn out every light in the station, but you have to hurry because they'll throw searchlights down here when they get high enough. You can take off in the confusion and slip away. When they come to investigate, I'll tell them I saved the station just in time and that you criminals escaped—how or where, I won't know."

As they left the room there came the roar of the police ships taking off.

"No worry about them!" cried Williams. "They're intent on saving their own precious necks."

Just as they reached the roof, every light went out. Manners had timed it exactly right. Under cover of darkness, they ran to their ship.

Hackworth, in the lead, jumped in. He waited impatiently for the others, but to his surprise, he heard Williams' voice.

"Start the motors, Earl, and get away from here as fast as you can. Head for home—and safety."

"What?" spluttered Hackworth. "And you—and Terry?"

"We'll take care of ourselves. No one knows you're connected with this. We've got to escape Unitaria, and we can do that without you."

"But, Dan—"

"Go, for Lila's sake! Hurry, Hackworth! Any moment the police will put a searchlight down here!" Hackworth shouted a good-by and took the ship up and away. To him it seemed a madman's move, but to have argued would have been futile. Hardly had he drawn safely away than hovering police ships, suspicious because the threatened catastrophe had not occurred, cast their lights downward. They revealed a deserted landing roof. The beams began to swing about frantically, but Hackworth was already beyond their effective range.

By the time the police had swung searchlights on the roof-top, Williams, Terry, and M'bopo were again in the control room, facing a startled Manners.

"The devil take you!" he cried. "You will get me in trouble now if the police find me with you."

"I've changed my plans," said Williams calmly. "Staying with Hackworth would have been dangerous, not only for us, but for him."

"You don't think about me!" cried Manners shrilly. "I helped you at great personal risk, and now you want me to hide you!"

"We're not going to stay, Manners," cut in Williams sharply. "Listen to me. I've heard that Iceland is an independent island where fugitives from the Unidum can safely hide. If we can get to Iceland from here—"

"You can't get transportation from this tide-station," cried Manners. "The nearest dock is at Long Island City."

"But you have planes here?"

Whatever Williams had in mind was never uttered, for the sudden harsh drone of laboring engines informed them that the police had returned.

Manners stared at them in speechless misery.

"Come on, Terry!" called Williams, racing to the door. "It was a mistake, not going with Hackworth. But we can still give the police a run-around."

It was senseless to think of going to the landing roof. Already they could hear the footsteps of approaching Unidum guards. Williams dashed down a corridor that led oceanward, Terry and M'bopo at his heels. There were shouts behind them. The corridor opened into a long and curving chamber from the opposite wall off which led straight passageways.

"This way!" said Terry suddenly, running down the hall. "There's a possible chance—"

At one of the long passageways whose end seemed lost in distance, he stopped and pointed at what seemed to be a miniature train.

"The tide-station's transportation system, propelled like an electro-car to the long tide-power piers, sometimes five miles long. I can run it!"

"Where does it lead to?"

"Well—nowhere. Out into the ocean."

"Come on," said Williams in sudden decision. "We'll take a ride in it. Perhaps somewhere along that five-mile stretch we can hide."

# CHAPTER X

Once they were all seated in the vehicle, Terry pulled the starting lever savagely. With but a faint hum of magnetic motors, it started, gathering speed swiftly, almost noiselessly on its rubber-covered wheels. But the enormously long cavern became resonant with the echoes.

The train ran on a ledge. Not twenty feet below was the ocean, swelling toward high tide. At high tide tremendous shutters would clip across the tide-pier dozens of feet down. The receding ocean level would then leave a great mass of water captured in reservoirs, and possessing terrific potential energy. How the weight of falling water was converted into kinetic energy, Williams could not see, nor did he care. All that interested him was how to get out of this predicament.

When the vehicle came to a stop before the end of the tide-pier, which was set with windows, they looked at one another in dismay. Behind them was the sound of another train.

"The police," said Terry emotionlessly, "are right on our heels. I suppose Manners had to give us away." He became suddenly vehement. "We're trapped, Williams! We've got a choice of capture and the Brain-control death, or—"

He pointed to the still, black water. It would be a quick and merciless death. He shuddered. Their brains! They would fish out the bodies and take out the brains—

"There is no escape. Williams, we—"

Terry felt a hand shaking his shoulder. An imperative voice was asking something. "Terry! What are those lights out there beyond the tide-pier?"

"Lights?" Terry looked. "Moored seaplanes—private craft mainly."

"Can you swim that far?"

"I'll try it," answered Terry.

They stripped to the skin and threw their clothes over the railing into the water. M'bopo went first through an opened window. Terry poised a moment before diving, shivering. Williams looked down the passageway, grimly. The police were still too far away to have seen what their quarry was doing. He closed the window hanging by the sill, then he dropped.

He came up gasping in the cold water. Calling softly to his companions, he struck out for the brightest of the lights which danced on the choppy water out in the gloom.

"Take it easy," he warned. "It looks like a long swim."

Terry changed to a smooth side-stroke. Williams littered a few dialect phrases to M'bopo. The Bantu pulled up to the side of the young chemist and let him set the pace. That this would be a test of stamina, Williams knew. And that Terry would be the first to weaken, he knew also.

They fought the ocean with its shoreward tow and chilling bite. Choppy waves seemed spitefully intent on choking them and pushing them under. It was an ordeal to test any man, and the bobbing lights ahead seemed to dance ever farther away.

It might have been an hour later—or a year, for all they knew—when Terry spluttered violently and stopped.

"I can't go on!" he gasped between clenched teeth and blue lips. "Maybe you can—make it—"

Williams and M'bopo swam to either side of him. "Here, Terry—one hand on each of our shoulders. Look, we're almost there!"

Terry had not the strength to raise his head and look. He held on to their shoulders grimly; under his aching fingers he could feel the rippling of powerful shoulder muscles. Could they go on much longer?

Ages later Terry felt a change in the motion of the swimmers. A voice that seemed miles away spoke.

"*Sarto!*" gasped Williams. "We've reached something."

Terry shook off his numbed lethargy and raised eyes that smarted from salt water.

"The sea-plane dock," he mumbled. "Climb up—rest."

Even as he said it, he wondered how it would be accomplished, for the floating dock's level was three feet above. He heard splashing and saw M'bopo leaping out of the water with frightful contortions in the attempt to catch the dock edge. He made it. With a spasmodic jerk that must have taken superhuman effort, he pulled himself up and rolled over onto the dock.

With the help of M'bopo reaching down, the other two men rolled onto the wooden surface. For minutes only stentorian breathing and spasmodic shivers occupied them as they lay flat, regaining their sadly taxed energy.

The dock was in reality a giant raft, anchored securely. Cut into its edges were spaces long and broad enough to admit the pontoons of seacraft. It was a public service for owners of seaplanes who wished to moor them temporarily. Each plane twinkled with red lights at the wing tips.

Williams was the first to stagger erect. He pulled Terry to his feet and made him jump around violently to restore circulation. M'bopo joined them. The exercise helped to revive them, even though the night breeze now threatened to freeze them.

"Let's go," said Williams, controlling chattering teeth with effort. "Must get a ship—fight for it. M'bopo—" He finished with dialect that brought a gleam to the Bantu's eyes.

In the deep gloom that lay over the floating dock, they made their way toward a tri-motored craft. Terry licked stiffened lips and worked tightened jaws.

"Williams, listen to me," he finally said. "They're moored with two ropes from pontoon-stays to dock-posts. Must loosen them."

Williams nodded. "But first we storm the cabin."

He cursed when they reached the first plane. Its cabin was dark and the doors locked. They went to the next and it, too, was empty and locked. At the third there was a light inside and the sound of many voices.

M'bopo looked inquiringly at Williams, who shook his head. A dozen or so men were more than they could handle.

The fourth was a small ship, twin-motored.

"Here we go," said Williams. "I'd rather fight than freeze."

He jerked open the cabin door and plunged in. Terry, crowding in after M'bopo, expected to hear shouts and cries, but all he heard was a muffled gasp and a crack of fist on flesh. Then he saw Williams grinning at him.

"Only one man," he said. "And I took care of him."

The cabin, comfortably heated, was bliss after what they had undergone. They relaxed in wordless ecstasy. The warmth gradually soaked into their blue skins and loosened their tongues.

"You can fly this?" Williams asked Terry.

"I think so. Controls look similar to landcraft."

"We must go as soon as possible. Unitaria is no place for us right now. I know"—Williams saw the frown on Terry's face—"that you are thinking of Lila, but we would be courting capture here. We can hide safely in Iceland, then do our best to get Lila there. That was why I wanted Hackworth to get away, so—"

He stopped short at a sudden sound of laboring plane motors—a ship landing. Terry, peering out on the dock, turned with dismay in his face.

"A police ship!"

Williams saw a striped ship bouncing to a stop near a housing whose windows were lighted. Five uniformed men leaped from the plane and banged on the door of the housing. The lone attendant of the seaplane mooring came out and they engaged in gesticulating conversation.

"Then the police are not so simple," muttered Williams. "They've come here on the chance we made this swim."

"The Unidum guards are noted for their efficiency," said Terry.

Williams saw the police head rapidly for the first of the moored craft, followed by the attendant. They disappeared in the shadows but emerged a moment later to walk toward the next plane.

"They're looking in each ship!" breathed Terry. "We've got to hide!"

"No use," said Williams quickly. "No place, anyway. Terry, start the motors and get ready for instant take-off. M'bopo and I will loose the moor-ropes."

"But they'll hear! With their lightning pistols, you two don't stand a chance—"

"Got to fight for it, Terry. You start the motors and leave the rest to us. If you hear me shout, give her the gun." He shot clipped Bantu phrases to M'bopo.

Terry opened his mouth to remonstrate, but they were gone. He thought of leaping out to help them, but decided to follow Williams' instructions. Williams seemed to have a peculiar knack for thinking of workable plans on the spur of the moment.

Terry grasped the starter switch and closed it. The twin motors hurled their powerful voice across the water.

Williams and M'bopo already had unhooked the mooring ropes from the pontoons. At a low-voiced command, the Bantu raced around the back of the ship to Williams and they crouched in the deep shadow of the wing nearest the police. They waited, eyes on the uniformed guards, like panthers at a zebra watering spa. Williams was transported back twenty years to a time when he and a brawny companion had ambushed a party of marauders under the shadow of a huge tree and routed them.

At the unexpected roar of the motors, the police whirled in surprise, lightning pistols in hand. They sprang forward, intent on capturing the outlaws before the motors were sufficiently warmed to start. As they raced past a wing to reach the cabin door two naked figures, one white and one black, leaped among them, hard fists flying.

The onslaught laid two of the guards out flat and senseless. The other three flung about with pistols upraised, to meet a storm of blows. One pistol flashed harmlessly into the night air, and its user crashed against the wing. His last impression was the shuddery one of a demoniacal face. The remaining two guards, knocked off their feet, bounced up again; but the weapons had flown out of their hands.

Williams and M'bopo began to take jolting punishment. Out of the corner of his eye, Williams saw the attendant stoop for one of the dropped lightning-pistols.

With a savage grunt, Williams lowered his head, and unmindful of a stunning punch from his antagonist, grasped him about the thighs and heaved mightily. He flung the helpless guard toward the attendant just as the man fired. The policeman sagged, paralyzed, and before the pistol spoke again, Williams had bowled over the attendant with a terrific blow to the chest.

He whirled to see M'bopo arising from where he had just squeezed the breath out of an adversary with scissored legs and strong fingers. "*Ulak g'nol*!?" He grinned. "Any more?"

Terry, sitting at the controls in apprehension, unable to hear a sound above the engine noise, heaved a sigh of relief as his somewhat battered companions appeared at the cabin door.

"Let's go," shouted Williams, "before more police ships come up!"

Terry pulled the ship gently along till the edge of the dock appeared, then opened the throttle. Then they were off the water and rising rapidly. Williams looked down at the dwindling dock and the huge tide-station on whose flat roof were numerous dots—the rest of the Unidum fleet. He suddenly laughed.

"We've given them something to think about," he said. "Can you find your way to Iceland, Terry?"

"I'll have to guess at it," admitted Terry. "But we'll find it. There's plenty of fuel—enough to go to Europe. We're safe now. But I wish I could be sure Hackworth got away safely."

"Beyond a doubt," said Williams confidently, then shook his fist in the direction of New York in a sudden reversal of thought. "Brain-controls, eh? Make us victims of the most inhuman thing ever seen on the face of Earth! Not while I—"

In the corner of his eyes he had seen the original occupant of the plane stir. The fellow sat up, rubbing a tender jaw. Williams was wondering what he would say.

He seemed about middle-aged, sturdy of body, and had remarkably penetrating dark eyes. Those eyes gleamed at Williams with dazed perplexity.

"I seem to have acquired a voluntary pilot," he said in a drawling voice.

"Yes, and two voluntary passengers, heading for Iceland. We mean you no harm. At our destination, we will give you back this ship."

"You are fleeing from the law?" queried the man, raising himself to one of the side seats.

"Which is no business of yours."

"And you were sentenced to death and the Brain-control?" the man asked.

Williams started. "You heard us... Well, as long as you know, what difference does it make?"

"Perhaps a lot," was the enigmatic reply. "After you get to Iceland, what then?"

"Don't tell him," warned Terry.

Williams scowled. "Whoever you are, you've got too much unhealthy curiosity. Just sit down and keep still."

He turned away and looked to the east. The first flush of dawn had changed the ocean to a sea of blood. The indistinct silhouette of an ocean liner was seemingly mired in the vast bosom of the sea.

Williams suddenly whirled. "Hold on there! What are you up to?"

The man, having arisen and taken a step toward the rear, halted and turned with surprise. "Why, you need clothes, don't you?"

"We do," retorted Williams. "But—"

"Watch him!" came from Terry. "He might have a gun in the supply room!"

# CHAPTER XI

Even as Terry spoke, Williams advanced on the original occupant of the seaplane threateningly.

"Just a minute," said the man. "We've got some things to talk over, I think. I've been trying to think just what to do, but now I've decided. I may be taking a chance with you three, but briefly, would you join an organization that will allow you to strike back at the Unidum?"

Williams stared, speechless. "What organization, and just who are you?"

"John Agarth is my name," said the man, coming closer to Terry so he could hear. "About a year ago, a group of men met in a small city of Europe and pledged themselves to a certain cause. To end the menace of the Brain-control!"

"Go on," said Williams breathlessly. "You can trust us."

"I do trust you," said Agarth. "I sense in you three a daring spirit we want in our members. To go on, the Brain-control, aside from its hideousness, is a distinct menace to humanity. It must be wiped out. Our organization, although large already, can still use men of spirit and daring. What is your answer?"

"Count me in," said Williams quickly, "and that includes my colleague here, M'bopo. Terry?"

"As an outlaw in the eyes of the Unidum," Terry said thoughtfully, "it would be unreasonable to refuse. But I reserve the right to pursue my own affairs if occasion arises."

"Reasonable enough," Agarth assured. "Now here's what I have to offer in return for your co-operation—immunity from the law in secret hiding places, and the opportunity of working out your own salvation. If our plans go through, the Unidum decree, which now demands your life, will be null and void. Then there will be the spice of adventure—"

"Which is most acceptable," said Williams.

"And for assurance that I am not deceiving you," continued Agarth, "look at this."

He pulled a folded paper from inside his coat. It was a Unidum criminal notice that John Agarth, as described, was an outlaw at large.

"You see," he explained at their surprise, "I once was sentenced to die, as you were, and to have the 'honor' of submitting my brain to a Brain-control. In the early days of our organization we were over-zealous, and made an abortive attempt to smash Brain-controls. Several of our members"—his voice was bitter—"were executed. The rest of us were rescued in a bloody jailbreak. From then on we planned more secretly and cunningly. We call ourselves the Brothers of Humanity. I will explain more in detail later. I think now you men had better sleep. I'll take the controls."

As he replaced Terry in the pilot seat, he rubbed his sore jaw ruefully.

"Williams, you gave me the surprise of my life at the floating dock. I was waiting for a secret word-of-mouth message from New York. I didn't expect a naked man to jump at me and knock me out."

"You understand—"

"Perfectly," assured Agarth. "The message will get to me eventually. Now instead of Iceland, we're going to our headquarters in Paris. It is secret, and safe."

Terry was already fast asleep on the floor. Before Williams succumbed he found a moment to revel in the thought of a pleasing future. What kind fate had saved him from the Unidum and brought him within reach of the opportunity to strike back? What to do about Lila? Unanswerable questions they were, that put him to sleep. Beside him lay M'bopo, more worn and battered than any of them, content that *Orno Akku* was still alive and free...

\* \* \* \*

In Paris, three days later, John Agarth came upon Williams and Terry talking together in a room of the secret headquarters of the Brothers of Humanity in Paris. "I have both good and bad news for you," Agarth said.

"From Hackworth?" queried Terry eagerly.

Agarth handed him a sheet of paper. "I got in touch with him through our secret communication channels. I've had the message decoded for you."

The gist of it was that Hackworth had made a clean escape from the police at the tide-station, that Lila was still peacefully sleeping to the exasperation of her doctors, and that Andrew Grant had admitted his absolute inability to get Lila's release from the Eugenics Law. Hackworth wanted to know what Williams and Terry planned to do next.

"I don't think there's any doubt about what we plan to do," said Williams. "We'll work toward the goal of the Brothers of Humanity. As long as Lila is safe, Terry, you can feel free to help. Let's see now... Lila has been in a coma for ten days. The Unidum's best medical men are puzzled and have failed to awaken her. The drug is beyond their knowledge."

"And only I," whispered Terry, "can awaken her!" He looked up at Agarth with shining eyes. "I pledge myself as a member of the Brothers of Humanity."

"Good," said Agarth. "And instead of merely becoming members without authority, each of you will be what we call 'marshal.' As you now know, the Brothers of Humanity has an orderly, semi-military foundation. At the head are the two generals. Next in authority are five majors, of which I am one. Then come the marshals, at present ten in number. Then come captains, lieutenants, and finally the brothers."

"But why should Terry and myself be honored?" asked Williams perplexed. "We haven't done a thing. We've just been a lot of worry and expense to you, Agarth."

"But you *have* done something," contradicted Agarth, smiling. He turned serious suddenly. "You have been instrumental, whether wittingly or not, in gaining two important members for our organization. Andrew Grant and Joe Manners!"

"They are now Brothers?"

"Yes. For some time our agents, who are constantly trying to enlist influential men, had been surreptitiously approaching both those men. Not till yesterday did either of them yield—Grant because Terry's plight had touched his heart, Manners because he suddenly saw how cruel the Unidum was in sentencing you two to death and worse. Grant and Manners are important additions to our Brotherhood, especially the man who controls the life-current that pours into New York."

"Manners is in no trouble because of us, is he?" asked Williams.

"No. There was suspicion and pressure against him at first, but the Unidum finally took his word that he'd had nothing to do with the escape of three 'vicious criminals.'"

Agarth left and Williams turned to Terry. "I can't begin to tell you how glad I am that events led to this, Terry. From the moment I heard that my sister's—brain—was in a Brain-control, I felt I could never know a moment of peace till I had done what I could to end her purgatory. And those hundreds of other brains! It's ghastly! Some kind fate has made it possible for me to help end the enslavement of the brains! To that I dedicate my every effort, and if need be, my life."

"And I, too," said Terry. "I find it hard to understand now how I ever resigned myself so abjectly to such things. For years the Brain-control where I worked had bothered me. Then when Lila was torn away from me by the Eugenics Law, I seemed to break like a dried reed. Only when you unfolded a plan to save Lila did I awaken from that mental lethargy. Now I see how mouse-couraged I was, and I'm determined to do my part to end this wrong."

* * * *

Three days before, Agarth had landed the plane on the shores of southern France—a state of Unitaria roughly corresponding to the France of pre-Unidum times—and they had been driven to Paris by agents of the Brotherhood, speeding along super-highways at two hundred miles an hour.

The new Paris with its spanned towers and spires and comfortable residences had shifted a few miles northward, leaving the old city deserted and falling to ruin. Now this old section, in one of the camouflaged underground strongholds of World War II, in use when a Hitlerized Germany occupied Paris, the Brotherhood had set up a headquarters, unmolested and unsuspected by the Unidum. The underground chambers were roomy and well-ventilated, an ideal habitation for men requiring utter secrecy.

Agarth and his agents had been gradually spreading the invisible web of the Brotherhood all over European Unitaria, working with four other centralized units in the continent. The superior headquarters of the Brotherhood, where the two generals of the organization guided the movement, was on the western coast of America near San Francisco.

The Brotherhood's main strength was concentrated west of the Rockies, where people had always been bitterly opposed to the usurpation of rights the Unidum had taken over.

The primary purpose of the organization of the Brothers of Humanity, as Agarth had said, was to end the enslavement of the brains. After their first sporadic attempt to smash all Brain-controls, which had ended so disastrously, Agarth and the others who had escaped had conceived a far better plan. To achieve it they needed a large membership of staunch adherents. Then, on a certain date, at a certain hour, members of the Brotherhood were to enter every one of the two thousand Brain-control chambers in Unitaria, and simultaneously ruin them by opening the nutrition boxes and injecting a virulent poison into the fluid pumped to the brains.

This, in itself, was merely a gesture, announcing that the Brotherhood had declared its existence to the Unidum. Then, with every Brain-control inert and useless, the Brotherhood was to arise and defy the Unidum ever to try again to set up Brain-controls. The Brotherhood was confident that public opinion would sway their way. They believed that the Unidum, suddenly confronted with such purposeful antagonism, and rather than precipitate a bloody revolution, would be forced to accede to the demands of the Brotherhood.

When Agarth joined Williams and Terry at dinner that evening, the conversation was about that day when the Brotherhood would drop its mask of secrecy and face the Unidum.

"Just how," asked Williams, "will the poisoning of the brains be done?"

"Well, that was one of our greatest problems," said Agarth. "It has to be done without a hitch. Only by demonstrating to all Unitaria that the Brotherhood is powerful can we hope to win. The news, 'ALL BRAIN-CONTROLS RENDERED USELESS. ORGANIZED GROUP DEFIES UNIDUM TO RENEW THEM,' will cause the majority of citizens to flock to our banner. But if we render useless only half or less of the Brain-controls, the Unidum will laugh at us and destroy us, knowing the people will have no confidence in us. That first move of ours must be complete and efficient.

"Sadly enough, this can only be accomplished at the sacrifice of many lives. Every man who goes to poison a brain on that great day will go a martyr! The only practicable way to destroy the brain in a Brain-control is by poisoning, and to do that the nutrition box must be opened. That opening will ring an alarm, so the poisoner will be captured. The Unidum will execute him summarily."

"Is there no way to open the nutrition boxes without ringing the alarm?"

Agarth shook his head. "The metal of the boxes is an alloy impervious to chemicals, to heat-torches, and to mechanical violence. The only way to get at the pump inside is via the lock and door. Since the lock is too intricate to pick, it must be forced. Each of our men on that day will have a small tool with spreading prongs which will be given a terrific leverage by means of a draw-screw. This, inserted in the keyhole that conducts electricity immediately rings the alarm. However, each man will have time enough to inject the poison before the guards come, but not time enough to escape! No other way of killing the brain is quick and sure enough to accomplish our purpose."

Williams and Terry had an identical thought.

"The acid, Terry!" cried Williams. "That eats steel!"

Terry nodded. "The lock mechanism must be of ferrous metal because the impervium alloy can't be machined that finely. The acid will eat it away in a wink!"

"Yes," agreed Agarth, "but acid carries electricity. The alarm will ring just as certainly as in the other case."

Terry leaped to his feet. "Not this acid! It doesn't carry current! It is a compound of helium and chlorine, as non-conductive as oil. At the merest contact with ferrous metals, it throws nascent chlorine loose, and frees helium."

"Strange," said Agarth. "I've never heard of that compound."

"It's a recent discovery," Terry said quickly, "not yet widely known or marketed. Only by great fortune did I have a bottle of it in my laboratory, which Hackworth knew about, and without which we should never have escaped prison."

Agarth sprang to his feet in excitement. "If it carries no current, then it is a godsend! It may mean the saving of many lives. Terry, we must get some of the acid and test it…"

\* \* \* \*

Arising from the water, a long, thin sliver of metal with wide, thin wings left France and soared gracefully into the rosy sky of dawn. Its motors sang a song of power. It ascended the crimson vault of heaven and when the air grew thin and cold, flaming gases belched from its rear, pushing it forward and upward mightily. In a grand arc, it puffed its way to the height of twenty miles, then leveled out, its speed so great that the dawn never broke into broad day to the occupants.

Inside the ship, Williams clutched the arm-rests of his seat, amazed at the powerful surges that pressed his body back against the leather. Agarth smiled a little, and Terry, at the other side, stared out the window, hardly less affected than Williams, although he had ridden in a stratosphere ship before. In a seat immediately back of them sat M'bopo, who while not terrified, was incoherent.

"*Sarto je Bru!*" muttered Williams. "I feel as if I'm going to Mars at a million miles an hour."

Agarth chuckled. "Everybody's first trip in a stratosphere rocket ship is terrifying."

They were bound for San Francisco and the main headquarters of the Brotherhood in one of the organization's rocket ships—the fastest mode of transportation known. Agarth had left the Paris headquarters in the hands of others. All the higher officers of the Brotherhood were now converging on San Francisco, to await the Great Day, only three days off. In Europe, hundreds of grim Brothers of Humanity awaited the zero hour when they would saunter into the Brain-control chambers as casual visitors and at a certain hour do the deed that was to end the Enslavement of the Brains.

In an hour, the rocket ship had reached its high cruising level. Artificial air pumped through the airtight cabin. Heating units hissed softly and kept out the cold. The pilots, after reaching a velocity of a thousand miles an hour, throttled the rockets to where they kept the speed constant.

Then it was easier for the passengers. Constricted chests were able to breathe naturally again.

"We will be there in seven hours," said Agarth. "Eight thousand miles in eight hours, counting the hour to ascend."

"And I thought the hyp-marine was fast!" commented Williams.

# CHAPTER XII

The panorama was awesome in its grandeur. The flush of permanent dawn suffused the scene with undulating billows of clouds. At times, a wide rift in the cloud-bank would unveil the shimmering green of endless ocean. Williams felt that he was looking at Earth from another planet. Around them the stars shone as brightly as light globes. And even when dawn slowly pushed the rim of the sun above water, the stars continued to shine defiantly.

"Some rocket ships have ascended as high as two hundred miles," said Agarth. "At that height, one is in space and the corona and halo of the sun fail to dim the stars."

"Have any rocket ships gone to the moon?" asked Williams.

"They have gone, but never returned. One unfortunate space pioneer fell into the moon's gravitational field to become its satellite. Astronomers can see his tiny ship swinging eternally in a narrow orbit—a wandering coffin."

At the mid-point of the ocean, Williams espied, through broken clouds, a sizable object apparently floating on the surface.

"*Sarto*, what is that?" he asked. "To be visible from this height, it must be a monstrous thing."

"That is a most cherished experiment of the Unidum Scientists," Terry observed. "There is a great deal of secrecy about it. It is supposed to be a plant to produce energy from sunlight, as sunlight already has been used for heating homes. The set-up of mirrors is on a raft a quarter-mile square. The mirrors collect the sun's rays not only from above, but from below—those reflected by the vast body of the ocean when the face of a wave turns right. At any one moment, countless square miles of wave faces reflect light to that setup. It collects them, and also the direct rays, and converts them into energy. It is still experimental, but the Unidum has high hopes of it. It has cost them years of labor and scientific effort. There are always dozens of Scientists aboard and skilled tradesmen."

"If the Unidum would only concentrate itself more on things like that," interjected Agarth, "instead of on an inhuman scientific mistake like the Brain-control, it would be all right. That sun-power affair, if it becomes practicable, can do only good."

"Unless they think of installing a few Brain-controls there too," said Williams.

High over the American continent flashed the rocket ship, once passing another and larger stratosphere plane. Williams could see by the way the towns and cities rolled down the horizon that they had a terrific speed. When the Rocky Mountains came in sight, the rocket blasts died out and the ship began to settle.

Agarth showed Williams how to turn his seat around to face the rear. He saw a good reason for that when the ship fell into heavier air and began to decelerate mightily.

Williams felt that a gigantic hand was pushing him up into the sky. For a half-hour they passed through swirling clouds. Then suddenly it was clear and Williams saw the ocean rise to meet them. A slight bump and swishing slide through water. Then silence.

"Here we are," said Agarth, springing up. "The Pacific in the first hour of dawn. We left at dawn and arrive at the same time!" He chuckled and opened the door, revealing a wooden dock. "We are a hundred miles from San Francisco. A brother is waiting to drive us to the Brotherhood's headquarters. There you will meet the two generals whose sagacity and zeal have made possible our crusade..."

\* \* \* \*

In the wilds of the Sierra Nevada Mountains, the Brothers of Humanity had set up their main headquarters in a hidden cave. There were no highways near, and from above, it was invisible. Supplies were brought in, and agents arrived and left in secrecy. Had the Unidum so much as suspected that such a nest of conspiracy existed, they would have borne down on it in full strength. That there had never been betrayal showed how cautiously and effectively the Brotherhood worked. A few potential traitors had been uncovered and disposed of.

As Agarth led them through passageways now and then a man passed, saluting Agarth. In several lighted rock rooms in the series of caves Williams could see men laboring with papers and codes and radio instruments. This was the core of the network of the Brotherhood.

Finally Agarth reached a room where a door had been built in. He knocked.

"Come in," said the man who opened the door. "The generals are expecting you."

At the far end of the large room several men sat at crude tables, writing. Against the wall was a desk at which sat two men who arose to meet them.

"Major Agarth, welcome!"

Agarth saluted, then turned to introduce Terry and Williams to Generals Hagen and Bromberg. Terry's eyes widened at the names.

"Hah!" said Bromberg. "You recognize us?"

"Y-yes," stammered Terry. "Professor Bromberg and Doctor Hagen were the two Scientists who wrote the monograph on the After-Life of Brains in the Brain-controls, and who were impeached and disappeared!"

"Exactly," agreed Bromberg. "Sit down, all of you." He went on: "Yes, we are those two Scientists. When we made our investigations and published the results we believed that would cause the abolition of Brain-controls. Instead, we were arrested, dragged into court like common criminals! We were exiled to Asia because Scientists cannot be executed by law.

"We labored there for the Federation of Asia as honored savants, but the disgrace of our banishment rankled, and we became more determined to end the enslavement of the brains. We heard of the attempt of Major Agarth and his men to smash Brain-controls, and got in touch with him after their sensational jail-break.

"The Brotherhood was organized. And three days from now, if fate wills, we will end the tyranny of Brain-Enslavement!"

Both Bromberg and Hagen were well past middle age. Bromberg was a man of grave demeanor, quiet and meek. Hagen was a fiery soul, excitable and talkative. His dark eyes gleamed with an almost fanatical light.

"Marshals Williams and Spath," Bromberg said, "we welcome you into our organization. Major Agarth has sent me relevant details about you in code. Doomed by the Unidum to be the victims of more insidious Brain-controls, you are doubly welcome. From the formula you sent for the new acid, we have already manufactured and sent bottles of it to all our agents in Unitaria. We will strike our first blow against the Unidum without their knowing it until it is too late even to apprehend the men who will poison the brains. The first they will know is that the machines in the food plants are acting strangely. They will investigate, perhaps not until hours after the poisoning. Ha! They will see the lock corroded—then they will know!"

Bromberg's eyes glistened. Then he turned to exchange a few words with Hagen.

"General Hagen wishes to confer with Major Agarth," he said. "If you, Marshals Williams and Spath, and your black man care to have lunch with me—"

They followed Bromberg to a nearby dining cave. Bromberg ran an approving eye over Williams.

"You are a brawny man, Marshal Williams. Agarth tells me you have been in Africa the past forty years. And your escape from the Boston prison and the runaround you gave the police, ha! Remarkable. Are you a man of luck, or great enterprise?"

"A man of quick wit and sudden plans," said Terry sincerely.

Williams flushed under his African tan.

"I think luck plays a great part in my life, General. Otherwise I should have been dead in Africa years ago."

Bromberg nodded. "I only hope you have brought some of your luck with you into the Brotherhood. Perhaps we'll need it… Let me tell you some things about the Unidum. I was in the Medical Bureau for years and learned a lot. The Unidum of today is heading towards tyranny and decay and the first signs of it are the Eugenics Law and the Brain-control innovation. When the Unidum came into being it was the greatest advancement civilization had ever known. Its members were the souls of integrity, the most intelligent, noblest of the entire federation. They founded a totally new type of government and gave it a hearty start.

"Then came the Eugenics Law, a wonderful idea but applied heartlessly and wrongly. Scientific eugenics may some day remodel the world, and people will be born more nearly equal, but a Eugenics Law which begins with tyranny only undermines the morality of all concerned. Loveless marriages are a return to feudal aristocracy with all its evils. Until ten years ago the Unidum worked like a clock, but after the passage of the Eugenics Law, there arose dissension. Many of the Scientists, Hagen and myself included, were opposed to the Law, but the other faction prevented us from doing anything. Then five years later, the second great blow fell—the enslavement of the brains!

"What the people do not realize, what even many of the Scientists do not realize, is what these things will eventually lead to—a cold, inhuman, scientific social system in which Scientists, rapidly increasing through the application of the Eugenics Law, will completely dominate a dwindling citizenship whose brains will go after death to run the machinery of the world! In a few centuries this will be a world of men who will call themselves Scientists but who will be slothful monsters, living like decadent gods in a completely mechanized world, falling to certain decay!"

The others listened as Bromberg continued.

"And the whole scheme originated in the mind of but *one* man—the present Executive Molier of the Unidum. He perfected the brain-rejuvenation process. He must have conceived his plans long before he became Executive. His co-executive, Ashley, is a puppet, powerless against Molier's superior will. Molier dominates Unitaria today. And by his persuasive powers, his subtle propaganda, he has begun the corruption of the once noble Unidum. If not checked, he will lead them to absolute tyranny and eventual decay."

Bromberg paused, then spoke with less passion.

"I see that these are unexpected revelations to you. Well, few outside of the Brotherhood have even the vaguest suspicion that a black cloud has darkened the future. You wonder too, how it is possible for one man to carry forward such plans. You must understand that the Unidum, in order to forge ahead rapidly with its Utopian principles, invested absolute authority in the central government. It controlled all industry. It limited private wealth. It supervised transportation and communication. And it gave to the two Executives dictatorial powers.

"With the People's Parliament dominated by Molier, it has been easy for him to get the Eugenics Law and Brain-control Act through. Yet so smoothly has he acted that he has made people believe that the Eugenics Law is commendable—more Scientists, more advancement. As for the Brain-controls—less work for the people.

"But the Unidum has not yet been corrupted. Once Molier's power is broken, all will be well."

"But after all," said Williams, "Molier is only a man. He must die some day. After his death won't his schemes puff away like a breath of foul air?"

"You don't know Molier," assured Bromberg. "He has foreseen that his ideals must live after him or his work is for nothing. He has poured poisoned words into the ears of many Unidum Scientists, painted a lurid picture of a future in which the unintellectual will not be around to hinder the advance of Science. It's easy to sway a Scientist with talk of scientific Utopias. His adherents form a sort of unorganized, yet powerfully growing group. Through Andrew Grant we have obtained their names. We even know who Molier has picked to succeed him. Professor Jorgen, a man no less cunning and ruthless than Molier, who—"

He caught the look of astonishment in the eyes of the new members as they heard the name Professor Jorgen. Terry quickly explained.

"Heaven forbid that she should marry such a fiend!" exclaimed Bromberg. "He, as well as Molier, must be stripped of all authority and power if Unitaria is not to become a vast experimental laboratory for Scientists. But only three days from now the Brothers of Humanity will bring them to an accounting..."

* * * *

The next day, after sober reflection on the matter, Dan Williams had a serious request to make, and put it up to Agarth.

"It is a decision I cannot make," said Agarth. "I'll have to refer it to one of the generals. Come on—we'll go see them."

They traversed underground corridors to the central office. Bromberg looked up from his papers with a tired smile.

"Sorry to disturb you at such a time," said Agarth, "but I must ask for your decision. Marshal Williams has requested to be delegated to the poisoning of the Boston Brain-control!"

Bromberg looked at Williams in surprise. "You wish to risk your life—"

"I do," said Williams, with determination. "In the Boston Brain-control is my sister's brain. Trying to smash the globe led to my sentence for treason—and Terry's. I've sworn to release my sister from that mental torture which you and Doctor Hagen have proved exists. I have done nothing noteworthy for the Brotherhood yet. In being one of the poisoners, I will have done my part."

"Marshal Williams," said Bromberg slowly, "I will not attempt to dissuade you, for I can understand your feelings. Let me shake your hand. You are a brave man."

Terry and Williams saw then how human the professor was. Before he had been merely an impersonal leader. Now his eye was moist with feeling.

"And I'd like to accompany Williams!" said Terry.

"Terry, no!" Williams was shaking his head.

"General Bromberg," said Terry. "Your answer?"

"Go, and God be with you! Such spirit as yours will save us from tyranny. Major Agarth, attend to the details."

They left General Bromberg then, and after an hour of instruction Agarth left them after a hearty hand-clasp. Terry, Williams, and M'bopo were escorted from the headquarters into a cold, clear night. A silent guide took them to an auto.

Reaching the coast an hour later, they were hurried to a waiting plane, a speedy Sansrun. In it they were to be taken to a small California city, to embark for Boston in a public airliner. Each of the agents sent out that night to poison the brains went from a different city. In Europe, the same careful system was employed.

Early the next day, two thousand members of the Brotherhood would simultaneously look at clocks, open the black metal nutrition boxes after destroying the locks, and pour a small vial of deadly poison into the jar from which liquid food was pumped to the brain in the globe.

# CHAPTER XIII

Some hours later Dan Williams and Terry Spath stepped from an electro-car in Boston.

"We are in constant danger of arrest," said Terry, "if anyone recognizes us as the men who not two weeks ago tried to smash the Brain-control." His eyes searched for the blue and red of Unidum police.

"I suppose so," said Williams, "but perhaps our very daring is our protection."

Passing a loitering policeman on the way to the food products building, Terry held his breath. Cold eyes fastened on them for a moment, then flicked aimlessly away. They were unrecognized! After all why should the Unidum guards be thinking only of those two men who had thrown a wrench in a Brain-control? Terry began to realize that it was only natural no police should stop them with an eye of suspicion. And as for entering food products, were there not visitors daily doing the same thing?

Yet the nearer they approached, the more nervous Terry became. He felt for the tiny flat aspirator in his inside coat pocket. Williams had in his pocket a vial of a virulent poison.

Early morning—it was only nine o'clock—had been picked for zero hour, since few sightseers were abroad at that time. The Brain-control room was empty when they entered it.

"Five minutes," whispered Terry. That closely had everything been planned.

Williams drew a long breath as he again gazed upon the globe which held his sister's brain. He felt a fierce exultation, but no hallucination that his sister was talking to him.

Williams spoke to M'bopo in dialect, then to Terry.

"M'bopo will watch at the far door. You stand at the near one. If all is clear, I'll go ahead. If not, we'll take the chance that all the other brothers are taking all over Unitaria and go through with it. Give me the acid."

Williams sprang lightly to the pit level. Calmly he inserted the aspirator nozzle in the keyhole of the black box and pressed the bulb. There was a sharp hiss. He glanced at the alarm bulb above; it was dark. He tried the handle. It stuck!

More acid with the nozzle twisting in his fingers. Louder hissing but still the handle would not turn! Keeping his eye on the alarm bulb, he sprayed again and again, till a strong smell of chlorinic substances pervaded the room. *Sarto!* What kept that half-destroyed lock from yielding? Beads of sweat were on his forehead. He wondered if the other brothers were having the same trouble.

A fierce whisper from Terry startled him. "Something coming! *Hurry!*"

Williams squirted the acid until it was gone, and desperately threw his weight on the handle. With a loud click it suddenly yielded. Swinging the door open, Williams stretched his hands toward the foremost of two jars, quickly unscrewed a threaded cap at the top.

"Good-by, Helen!" he murmured, as he dropped the gelatin vial into the jar. "It is for the best!" The action of water on the gelatin would release the poison.

Williams swung the door shut and turned, ready for anything.

"Up here quickly!" whispered Terry. "They don't know—"

Two elderly women who had entered, loudly telling each other all about the Brain-control, were too busy to notice two flushed, excited men. Waving to M'bopo to join them in the corridor, Williams and Terry left.

It had worked perfectly. It might be hours before the erratic behavior of the machines below would be detected. They left the building as calmly as they could and in a few minutes stepped from the escalator onto an electro-car platform.

Williams felt as though a great load had been lifted from his shoulders. "It is done! It is done!"

Those words revolving in his mind brought him a deep peace.

Then Terry had grasped his arm and was pulling him toward one side of the platform. "Didn't you hear me, man? I said I'm going to call up Hackworth, tell him we've succeeded, and ask about Lila!"

Terry stepped into a phone booth while his companions waited outside. He emerged with a happy smile on his face.

"Lila! She's still 'sleeping' soundly! Hackworth was overjoyed to hear my voice. He wanted us to come see him but I told him it would be inviting disaster."

"Right. It won't be healthy for us in Boston, or anywhere in the East in a few hours. We must get to the West Coast."

At a shout they whirled, startled. A man in blue and red uniform was tugging at his lightning pistol and running toward them. Two other guards at the far end of the platform were racing up.

"We're recognized!" gasped Terry.

Williams swept an eye over the scene. The long, narrow platform, with few people in sight, was a bad place to be confronted by police. Yet the escalator was too far away for them to make a run for it. Far down the tunnel-like span he could see an approaching electro-car— and there were only three guards!

Williams whispered rapidly. M'bopo nodded, with a fierce grin. Terry set his jaw grimly.

The guard who had first shouted hurled explanations to the two who came up. They ran to where the three men waited quietly.

"You're under arrest!" cried the one in the lead. He waved his pistol threateningly. "Better come quietly."

"Just a minute," said Williams. "What have we done?"

A small crowd quickly formed about them. The police waved them back.

"You're Dan Williams and Terry Spath, wanted for treason and jail-breaking," declared the guard, though somewhat puzzled by Williams' calm. "I recognize you all right!"

"Such insolence!" exclaimed Williams, looking insulted. "Do you hear that, Briggs?" He turned to Terry. "We are those arch-criminals who tried to wreck a Brain-control!" He faced the guard sternly. "Sir, out of three million people in Boston did you have to pick out us for your horse-play! I shall report you!"

The guard lowered the pistol in indecision. The other guards who had merely answered their companion's shouts, looked embarrassed at the crowd's laughter.

"Well, I must do my duty," said the accusing guard doggedly. "You look like those criminals. I'll have to ask you to come with me to the nearest police office for a check-up."

"Shall we allow this fellow to disgrace us?" Williams asked Terry. "Or shall we"—the electro-car was hissing to a stop—"*give them what they deserve?*"

The three of them leaped forward suddenly. Three hard fists knocked three uniformed men flat, without a chance to raise their pistols.

The crowd scattered in alarm, some toward the escalator, others stampeding into the electro-car, with Williams and his companions among them. It was an automatic transfer station, so there was no conductor to raise an alarm. The driver, seeing nothing of the fracas, sent the electro-car humming away from the platform on which lay three prone figures. One of them staggered erect, shouting futilely for the car to stop. Then he picked up the other two guards, and raced for the phone booth.

Inside the electro-car, Williams, Terry, and M'bopo grinned as they sat down near the exit. Those who had witnessed the affair looked terrorized, as though expecting them to begin a general massacre. The rest of the passengers looked avidly curious.

"Safe for the moment," breathed Williams. "But they'll be on the lookout for us. We *must* get out of Boston and the sooner, the better."

"They'll have guards at *every* station on this line before long," Terry said hurriedly. "If we transfer at the next automatic transfer station to a lower level line, we'll slip out of their hands, because they can't have guards at every station in the city."

Williams pulled something from his pocket and thrust it into Terry's hand without revealing it to nearby passengers. Terry felt the smooth outline of a lightning pistol.

"I picked up one for you and one for me," explained Williams. "How do you work them?"

"Button on the side where you hold your index finger," said Terry. "But be careful with it! The catch near the firing button has two positions—one for a paralyzing charge, the other for a killing charge. And if we ever get caught with these—"

Williams smiled. "You forget we're already criminals under a death sentence. Pistols can't make us worse felons."

Terry jumped up, releasing his seat-hands, as the electro-car came to a halt.

"Come on! We transfer here."

They leaped out the door.

Williams glanced hastily up and down the platform and breathed in relief. Not a policeman in sight. Terry led the way to an escalator. At the next lower level he turned into a banistered walk that took them to the middle of one of three platforms. An electro-car stopped before them. As they entered it a blue and red figure dashed from the escalator opposite, waving and shouting. But the electro-car whisked away.

"They're on our trail," Terry said. "To fool them we'll skip the next station and stop at a terminal. We'll pay another fare, and take an express."

There were no shouting guards at the terminal, and the three embarked safely on a sixth-level span car. It rumbled on its grooves at frightful speed.

"*Now* let them locate us with three misleading transfers between us," Terry smiled grimly.

"Now how do we get out of Boston?"

Terry was silent in thought for a moment.

"At the next transfer station, I'll take a look at the city guide. Frankly, I don't know where we are. Then we can get to an airport and—" He frowned. "Williams, word will have been received by now at every airport to watch for us. We don't stand a chance of getting aboard without being stopped. Every train depot will have notice, so will the hyp-marine depots and docks. There's only one way left to get out of the city, unless we walk, and that's by automobile."

"Then by auto it is," said Williams.

"But there's no public service in autos. They are all owned privately. We would have to—to confiscate one."

"That shouldn't stop us," returned Williams with a shrug.

An hour later found them in the west suburbs of Boston, watching the sparse morning auto traffic and the occasional pedestrians. A cool breeze swept upon them. They shivered, for their clothing was designed for warmer temperatures.

"It's not so easy," Terry was saying pessimistically. "We can't jump into a moving car, and those parked are sure to be either locked or without the ignition key."

"Can't we hire a taxi and throw the driver out?"

"Taxi? What is that?" When Williams explained, in surprise, Terry shook his head. "We don't have such things, Williams. People either use electro-car service, or own their cars."

"*Je Bru il Bra!*" exclaimed Williams. "Well, we can't go back downtown, with a horde of vultures in blue and red scouring around for us there. And once they find out that the Brain-control is poisoned, and hear that all the Brain-controls in Unitaria have been tampered with, Unidum guards will be looking with suspicion at everybody."

Williams moved away.

"We've got to find an auto with keys. Perhaps if we look into all parked cars, we might find one waiting for us to jump into and go."

An hour of searching did no good. Williams began to grip the pistol in his pocket tightly and cast his eye at slow-moving autos.

He felt his arm gripped by spasmodic fingers. It was Terry.

"Listen!"

They had reached one of the public open-air Newsmarkets, set off from the street and large enough to seat a hundred persons. From fan-grouped loud-speakers came the stentorian voice of the announcer.

"Boston Brain-control ruined! The brain in the globe has been poisoned! Two women found there tearfully deny having anything to do with it. They claim three men, one of them a Bantu, were leaving as they arrived. The three were accosted at electro-car Station Level Four Number Ten and fled after attacking three Unidum guards. The lock on the nutrition box—"

The announcer went into detail while Terry and Williams looked at one another aghast. Already a swift crowd had jammed the Newsmarket.

"Let's get out of this vicinity!" muttered Terry. "Now we are in for it."

As they hurried away the giant voice was saying:

"—reports from New York, Philadelphia, and Pittsburgh that the Brain-controls in those cities have been poisoned! This seems to be the beginning of an anti-Unidum move—"

"Not to mention what Professor Bromberg and Doctor Hagen will be broadcasting to Unitaria soon." Williams smiled grimly. "Terry, follow me, and don't be afraid to use that pistol if you have to!"

Williams had seen an auto stop before a house a hundred feet away. Out of it stepped two men who looked in surprise at the men running at them.

"We need your car," snapped Williams.

"What is this?" spluttered a tall powerfully built man.

"Hand over the key," grated Williams. "We want your car and we'll fight for it!"

The man swung a fist that missed. Then he backed away at the sight of the pistol Terry was aiming at him.

"Your key!" said Terry.

Reluctantly it was handed over. "I'll have you jailed for this!"

"Better men than you have tried it!" sang out Williams from the auto, as it hummed away from the curb.

# CHAPTER XIV

Grimly intent, Terry drove as swiftly as he dared, winding along the streets till he struck the highways outside the city. At noon they reached Worcester and took passage on an airliner to San Francisco. There they contacted one of the Brotherhood's undercover agents, and were driven by auto to the general headquarters. It was close to midnight when they entered the secret underground passages.

The guide led them directly to Agarth who greeted them warmly.

"I have been wondering about you all day," he said. "When Stevenson phoned—secret radiophone—from San Francisco that you were on the way here, I was relieved. I feared the Unidum had you."

"It was close," said Williams, and recounted the adventures of the day. "How has it all turned out in general?"

"Splendidly!" cried Agarth, eyes aglow. "Every Brain-control in Unitaria except a possible three, is useless! Reports from Europe have been coming in all day. And our American agents have come back alive and successful. There are only three Brain-controls we know nothing about, for the operatives assigned to them have not arrived or phoned. They may have failed and been captured, or killed by guards in escaping. However, we can claim success. Already public newscasts have hinted that a gigantic revolution is on. The Unidum as yet has made no official move."

Agarth turned back to his work.

The next morning Terry and Williams met Bromberg in a corridor. Pre-occupied and careworn though he looked, he stopped to greet them.

"I heard about your safe arrival from Major Agarth," he said. "We're proud of you, as we are of all our operatives against Molier and his tribe. Ha! Two thousand brains know a peace that has been denied them for five long years! If we accomplish nothing else, at least we have done that. Yet we will accomplish much more. I *know* it! Quiet citizens who have long hated the Enslavement of the Brains, but have never dared protest, are gaining courage. The Unidum will find the mob growling at any attempt to call it treason. This afternoon we will thunder it to all Unitaria!"

He left Terry and Williams with the firm conviction that unless unforeseen circumstances thwarted him, he would surely take the threat of tyranny from Unitaria.

At a conference called the next day, for the opening announcement of the Brotherhood's further plans, Williams took in the scene with interest. It was a large rock-bound chamber far below the ground level. Near one wall on a wooden dais were the two generals. Hagen was sitting quietly, in deep thought, Bromberg was pacing up and down, hands clenched behind his back. On a table near him was a microphone, its red signal dark. Grouped about the dais were all the officers of the Brotherhood then in America, grim-faced. The atmosphere was tense.

Agarth stopped beside Williams and Terry.

"We're waiting for connection to the Universal Broadcast System," he informed them. "It will carry Bromberg's speech to every corner of Unitaria."

"Isn't it dangerous doing that?" asked Williams. "Suppose the Unidum traces the wave and decides to crush the Brotherhood?"

"They can't trace the wave," informed Agarth. "We have not gone ahead blunderingly. From here Bromberg's voice will be carried by *wire* to an amateur ham's broadcasting antennae far to the east. From there it will connect to some sub-station of the Universal Broadcast System. At any moment now, one of our brothers who are radio staff men will complete the connection."

"Are these underground strongholds unknown to the people at large?"

"In the main, yes. Most of our hideouts are located in barren spots. Still the Unidum will not be able to ignore us because our very existence means revolution. And—"

Agarth stopped as the red signal light on the microphone began flashing brightly. General Bromberg took a position before it. A small man whose dark eyes gleamed in a careworn face, Bromberg's voice rang out in words that were to change history.

"Citizens of Unitaria! Since our ultra-nation came into existence, under the leadership of a scientific government, it has been known as the Unidum. 'Uni' from unity, and 'dum' from *duma* or power—the power of unity! United in common interests and privileges, the civilization of Europe and America has been tremendously advanced. With petty national animosity eliminated, with a standard tongue replacing the confusion of dozens of languages, with every state working toward the common good, and with a central governing power both strong and sagacious, Unitaria unquestionably is the best and greatest community of human beings of all time.

"But a crisis is upon us! Citizens must now decide between passive acceptance of governmental mistakes, or active resistance to them. Foremost among such mistakes is the Brain-control Act. I, Professor Bromberg, and my colleague, Doctor Hagen, exiled three years ago by the Unidum, declare to all the world that the Brain-control Act is more hideous and heinous than the Spanish Inquisition! Every unfortunate brain used to run machinery like a mechanized robot, although dead medically, lives an after-life of perpetual agony! Memories of life, subconscious impressions of their slavery, and a desire for release, torture those brains every minute of every day. The Unidum will deny it, but it is true!

"The Unidum will tell you that the use of dead brains will make life for the living easier and pleasanter, will increase leisure time, and make life free and happy.

"Yes, but think, citizens of Unitaria! Think of a future in which Brain-controls run all machinery. Then think of a purgatory after life in which your enslaved brain, remembering, labors hour after hour for years on end! *You* would then pray for death—and it would be denied you. What good to live a life of ease and plenty when the price is a horrible nightmare from which there is no release until the very nerves of your brain burn out from torment? What good to live like a god when the death that comes eventually is merely a door to a more dreadful Hades than even Dante could have described?

"Yet the Brain-control Act is an official statute. The Unidum has defended it tenaciously even though its inhumanness has been demonstrated. It was foreseen that there must be organized opposition. Doctor Hagen and I are the heads of an organization pledged to end the enslavement of the brains! We appeal to you, citizens, to help bring the Unidum to realize its terrible mistake.

"We, the Brothers of Humanity, have taken the initial step. Yesterday, as doubtless all Unitaria knows by now, our operatives poisoned every brain in every Brain-control in our land. *And brains must never be used again*! The Unidum must be made to realize, by petitions, notices, mass opinions, that no longer can we tolerate such an evil as the use of brains in machinery. It is up to you, citizens of Unitaria, to complete what we have begun. No government, however powerful, can ignore public opinion.

"I will not speak for our Brotherhood again unless conditions require it. Do not forget, however, that we are highly organized and absolutely determined to end the enslavement of the brains!"

Bromberg turned from the microphone to be greeted with lusty cheers.

"My friends," Agarth said to Williams and Terry, "that speech will go down in history. No matter how the Unidum may try to suppress it, it will live by word of mouth."

"You think it will be suppressed?" asked Williams.

"Certainly. It was only by a trick that it was broadcast today, an elaborate trick in which our operatives opened the broadcast channels for the few minutes that Bromberg talked. From now on the Unidum will guard the broadcast channels like a hawk, and will see to it that no printed copies are circulated. Bromberg expects mass opinion to carry the day, but I—well, some will hesitate, some shrink at the thought of opposing government. Others will wait to see what somebody else does. I don't believe the Unidum will abolish Brain-control without—bloodshed!"

* * * *

He was right. The next day an official answer was given by the Unidum to the document demanding repeal of the Brain-control Act. The Unidum decree stated that Professor Bromberg and Doctor Hagen and their compatriots were guilty of treason and were rebels, to be hunted down as such.

On the third evening after the broadcast Agarth dropped in on Williams and Terry in their cave room. He was in a fever of excitement.

"Everything is topsy-turvy," he said, nervously lighting a cigarette. "Unitaria is in an uproar. The people have begun to squabble, for the Unidum has been dispensing verbal poison. Our statements have been refuted, facts distorted, we've been called anarchistic rebels seeking power, and investigations that will soon be sending hundreds to death without trial for treason have been begun. Even Bromberg is beginning to admit that Molier has achieved more massive control than any of us thought. He has placed himself on such solid ground that nothing short of assassination or revolution will shake him loose. In war the Unidum was conceived. Must it die that way too?"

Agarth sighed and stood up.

"A general meeting of all officers has been called. Come."

The great room with the dais was even more crowded than it had been on the day of the broadcast. Practically every officer of the Brotherhood was there, many having come from Europe at the signs of brewing trouble.

Bromberg raised a hand for silence and addressed the officers.

"As you all know," he said, "the Unidum has struck back powerfully. Executive Molier is playing for high stakes. He has organized the Scientists whom he has baited with lust for power, and that group holds the entire Unidum in its grasp. With Jorgen as his first lieutenant, he is organizing an offensive against us.

"And, Brothers of Humanity, we must defeat him! We will be fighting the power of the whole Unidum, but we will soon have thousands flocking to our banner. In a few days we will have a completely equipped broadcast station set up and through it the mobilization of our military forces will begin. Our first move must be to take over the whole Western coast as base territory, and we will be striking ahead of the Unidum. The Pacific hyp-marine fleet is ours now. The crews of over half the fleet are ready to renounce the Unidum. We have secret underground strongholds from Vancouver to Mexico. The Federation of Asia will supply us with armament.

"It will mean hard work, men—bitterness and bloodshed. We are not fighting the Unidum's principles of peace and cooperation—we are pitting ourselves against Molier! Ostensibly, we are enemies of the Unidum, but we are seeking to break Molier's power, not to disrupt Unitaria. And we will press our campaign until public opinion demands repeal of the Brain-control Act. Once the people see the connection between the Eugenics Law and the Brain-control Act, nothing can prevent the downfall of Molier.

"But we must work fast. Molier realizes his predicament. Each of you officers report to Major Agarth by midnight tonight for assignment to definite work. General Hagen and myself, with the majors, go into immediate conference."

# CHAPTER XV

Uneasy and worried, once Williams and Terry were back in their room, Terry wiped a perspiring brow.

"Whew! War! Revolution! And the suddenness of the whole thing! The utter secrecy with which the Brotherhood worked!"

"They had to, Terry," Williams said, "with as powerful and watchful a government as the Unidum. That's why the first blow struck had to have such a staggering effect. What armament does the Unidum possess, Terry?"

Terry sat down and drew a chair close to Williams. "The equipment of today," he explained, "is not much different from that used in the All-Nations War, except that they did have A-bombs and H-bombs then, which now have been outlawed, and are no longer produced. Besides, between the super-nations of today there's armed peace. Unitaria has several fleets of armed hyp-marines that take the place of the battleships and dreadnoughts. She has also a sizable fleet of bombing and fighting aircraft. Little ground artillery has been manufactured since the last war. Frankly, the Unidum is little better prepared for warfare than we are."

"But suppose," suggested Williams, "they swept their air fleets across the Rockies and cruised hyp-marine fleets on the coast? Couldn't they squeeze us into defeat?"

Terry shook his head vehemently. "You remember Bromberg saying Asia will supply us with armament? The Unidum fleets will meet fleets of our own. As for the hyp-marines, the Pacific fleet seems ready to join us right now. The Brotherhood must have made particular efforts to influence those crews."

Williams thought a moment. "I can only hope for the best."

Suddenly Terry's eyes flashed. "Don't you see, Williams? If the revolution is successful, not only the Brain-control Act will go by the board, but also the Eugenics Law. Lila will be saved. When peace is restored I'll be free—and Lila will be free!"

Williams nodded.

* * * *

A cold October wind chilled Williams as he stepped from the warm interior of an auto and crossed a stretch of rocky ground at the heels of a silent guide. Revealed in the moonlight were mountains to the east. They trudged on, zigzagging around rocky barriers until there loomed before them an immense boulder with a queer shape. At one side of it the guide thumped the ground with his heavy boot. It sounded hollow.

Suddenly and mysteriously, the boulder rolled away from an opening in the ground from which streamed a dim light. Williams smiled as he saw a lever arm extending from the pit to the inside of the cardboard "boulder." It was something original in the way of camouflaged underground entrances.

"The password," mumbled a voice from the pit.

"'Liberty in life and death!' Marshal Williams to see Major Agarth."

As Williams clambered down the wooden steps, the man below saluted and pulled the level that swung the imitation boulder into place.

"This way, sir. Major Agarth is expecting you." Descending inclines brought them to a door labeled "Headquarters."

"How are you, Williams?" cried Agarth, springing up from his map-strewn table. "You look well—thinner though."

"And tougher." Williams laughed. "The past two weeks of flying and jumping around have put me in physical trim."

"You seem to be enjoying all this," said Agarth.

"I like to be in the right and to fight for it," agreed Williams.

"Let me congratulate you on your recent Nevada coup, Marshal Williams. Where did you ever conceive such a brilliant move?"

"Africa taught me that, Major," Williams said. "When a large force of Zulus once threatened to break through my meager line of Bantu warriors, I tried a simple trick, confident that their ferocity would overcome their judgment. At dawn, half my warriors sneaked by the Zulu encampment, purposely careless. The enemy pursued with triumphant shouts. But they changed to howls of alarm when the other half of my zealous Bantu plunged into their rear. In the Nevada skirmish, I did the same thing, substituting Unidum ships for Zulus, and our own craft for Bantu warriors. Then the anti-aircraft guns at Desert Point picked them off by the dozen."

"You speak lightly, yet if the Unidum fleet had broken through there, Base Number One would have been open to attack. General Bromberg made a wise move in appointing you squadron commander of the Nevada fleet."

Williams waved a deprecating hand.

"Thank you, Major. I have only done my best, which is what every Brother of Humanity is doing."

"Yes," said Agarth, haggardly. "But how little we have gained! So far, we have been on a desperate defensive. No loss is small gain, they say."

"After all, the moral victory is ours so far," Williams assured. "The Unidum boasted it would crush the rebellion in one week. *Two* weeks have passed and no fleet of theirs has crossed the Rockies to stay. And that naval battle three days ago! The Unidum Atlantic fleet retreating after losing two ships!"

"Only because the Unidum realized the foolhardiness of pressing forward at great loss. The Federation of Asia only too eagerly watches the internal strife of Unitaria. Some of them would greatly relish a chance to regain the 'face' they lost after their thorough defeat in World War Two."

"What reports from our propaganda operatives?" asked Williams.

"There we have more optimistic tidings," returned Agarth, brightening. "The public, through our literature which exposes Molier, Jorgen and their company, is fast being organized by our agents, and prepared to present a weighty petition not only to cease the civil warfare, but demanding a Unidum impeachment. Europe is muttering against Molier. Street-corner speakers in New York are denouncing him. Williams, if we can hold out another two weeks, Molier will be a broken despot!"

"Then we'll hold out," Williams said confidently. "If you hold your corner up here in Oregon so that coming through Canada is blocked for them, and I my niche down in Nevada to block off a sally through Mexico, the Unidum won't find a crack to crawl through to get to our West Coast stronghold. Kessel, Brighton and Walter have held the front along the Rockies without a sign of weakening."

Agarth nodded. "Hold out two weeks—just two weeks!" He changed his tone. "How is young Spath and that Bantu friend of yours? What do you call him—Umboko—Mopoto?"

Williams chuckled. "Young Spath's fine. Has a good head on him, and he's helped me make some vital decisions. I left him in charge to come here. M'bopo is my aide. He's outside in the car."

When a sharp buzz sounded, Agarth tripped the radio-phone lever. "Major Agarth speaking."

"Hello, Major," came from the loud-speaker. "General Bromberg. Has Marshal Williams arrived there yet?"

"Yes, he's here now."

"Ah, good. Then listen to me, both of you." The voice became excited. "Flash report from Operative B-Sixty-six in New York. New offensive planned by the Unidum. Large fleets preparing for attack at every point of the front—at dawn tomorrow. We must plan defenses, hold them at all costs."

After taking part in plans for repelling a formidable attack by the Unidum forces, Dan Williams rushed back to his fleet.

* * * *

"Terry, it looks bad," said Williams as their plane, the flagship, led the fleet to a temporary refueling center in southern California. "That titanic mass attack two weeks ago by the Unidum marked the turning point. Up till then we held them on the other side of the Rockies. Now Agarth has been pushed south, our eastern front has buckled, and we have been shoved north from the Mexican border. If the squeezing continues, our defeat is inevitable."

"But our underground strongholds! They are impregnable from air attack. As long as we hold them—"

"If we hide in them, the enemy can starve us out. The underground strongholds are fine for infantry bases, but in aerial warfare like the Unidum has launched, they are white elephants.

"Molier must have realized at once that if he gave the Brotherhood time to recruit a large infantry, the civil war might be drawn out to great lengths, because the entire West Coast could have been cut off from Unitaria. So he attacked swiftly with air forces. It's only been a month since the start of the revolution, and already the campaign is coming into its final stages."

"But surely all hope isn't lost for us?"

"No. If the tide of public opinion sweeps high enough, the Unidum will be forced to arbitrate. And any sort of arbitration is a victory for the Brotherhood. Indications are that already the Unidum—or rather Dictator Molier—is at odds with public sentiment. His authority is near a break. That's why he's pressing us so ferociously. If he can defeat us quickly enough, he will be doubly powerful, probably oust Executive Ashley and become sole dictator."

The radio-phone buzzed, and Williams picked up the receiver. He listened, then turned a grave face to Terry.

"The Unidum has effected its blockade of the Pacific. We are cut off from Asiatic ammunition and war supplies."

"But our hyp-marine fleet—"

"Can do nothing," finished Williams. "The Unidum has concentrated almost its entire hyp-marine forces in the Pacific. And—Molier has bought off the Federation of Asia!"

\* \* \* \*

In the largest chamber of the main underground stronghold in the mountain wilderness all the highest officers of the Brotherhood were assembled for emergency council.

The Unidum had relentlessly driven the rebel forces inward from the north, south, and east. The large fleets of the Unidum held at bay the rebel fleets which had not been reinforced from Asiatic channels for a week. All general merchandise air traffic had been halted. Supplies, especially fuel for war-craft, were increasingly hard to obtain for the revolutionists.

Throughout Unitaria feeling against the Unidum was running high, and there was a growing demand that warfare cease and the government accede to the demands of the Brotherhood. But Molier refused to listen, and had fortified the capital with anti-aircraft guns and war-craft. This step bid fair to disrupt Unitaria, for Europe was prepared to secede at a moment's notice.

Molier had but one thought—to crush the rebellion and take control. His co-plotters, Scientists, some of whom fervently wished they had never listened to him, as many of those who had supported Hitler felt, when they were too deeply involved to back out, held control of authority and issued the orders which daily drove the rebels backward.

Yet the responses to military commands were not as prompt as they should have been. Even the plane crews, long trained to obey orders without question, were sulky.

General Bromberg, broken and haggard, walked up and down the dais, haranguing the Brotherhood officers fitfully.

"Blasted hopes are all we have left, Williams," he said to the marshal, sitting beside him.

"Some of us still have the spirit to fight," said Williams.

"Fight?" Agarth replied wearily. "For what? Victory now would be bitter irony. Europe is ready to secede and is arming to fight the Unidum. Molier has embittered the very name Unidum for people everywhere."

"But if Molier and his crowd were out of the way, couldn't the Unidum regain its former prestige?"

"Who knows?" Agarth said blankly. "All Unitaria has been undermined. There is rioting every day in big cities. The Brotherhood's proclamations and Molier's propaganda have become confounded in the mass mind until nobody knows which is what."

"But an uncorrupted Unidum—wouldn't that cure all evils?"

"Certainly," replied Agarth a bit sharply. "But here are we, doomed to certain defeat. And with us dies that leadership that could have saved Unitaria from Molier and tyranny. With the Brotherhood destroyed, Molier will despotize Unitaria or plunge Europe and America into a war that will be ten times worse than this one we have gone through."

Williams mused for a moment. "Molier—tyranny. No Molier—no tyranny."

"What's that you say?" queried Agarth.

Williams eyed him a moment. "Molier is human. If he were assassinated then—"

"Are you mad? The capitol has been fortified. Molier has had a bodyguard since the beginning of the revolution. You would have to be a magician to kill him."

"Then I'll be one! Agarth, I want your authority and permission to leave base here. Give me ten fast ships and twenty men, and full tanks of fuel."

# CHAPTER XVI

Dumbfounded, Agarth stared speechlessly at Williams. It was at the tip of his tongue to ask Bromberg's advice, but one look decided him otherwise. After all, what difference would it make? The ten ships and twenty men could not hold out to the end, anyhow.

Agarth nodded. "Go if you will."

"I am coming along," said Terry who had stood by silently.

Williams looked into his eyes. "Of course," he agreed, "and M'bopo too. This might be our last great adventure together."

"How will we get past the Unidum lines?" asked Terry, as they left the room.

"Fly over. I doubt they'll pursue. Likely will figure we're deserters."

A swift plane took them to a landing where they were in the midst of what remained of a formerly great fleet, Williams' own fleet that he had commanded for four hectic weeks.

The word flew from tent to tent that the commander wanted to speak to his men on some mysterious matter. When they were assembled Williams looked them over with pride. These were the men with whom he had held the frontier against the Unidum. They had no uniforms, but on the breast of each was pinned the silver and blue enamel emblem of the Brotherhood. And in each face still was an eagerness and determination.

"Men, I need some of you tonight," shouted Williams, "on a mission of great danger. We are ringed in by the enemy and it is only a question of hours before the final battles. Our leaders are planning the last desperate defensive. But daring may sometimes accomplish what might cannot. I want twenty men to come with me—to New York!"

Confused murmurs quickly became cheers. Then a man's bellowing voice roared: "Why can't we all go along, Commander, if you're figuring on storming the capitol?"

"No!" shouted Williams against an approving babble. "Ten ships have a chance to cross the enemy lines where the fleet would not, without becoming engaged in a battle to the finish. And this is a strategic move. Numbers will not help."

Men began crowding forward to be chosen. Williams looked at Terry.

"Take only those who are not married," suggested Terry.

Williams immediately shouted for all married men to return to their tents. They did, with some murmuring. Williams looked over the thirty-odd men, picked out his twenty, and in another half-hour, eleven ships with full tanks arose with a roar of helicopter screws. Under radio-phone command from Williams' ship, they separated widely and bored swiftly eastward, climbing steadily.

In their own plane, Terry was in the pilot seat while Williams sat before the radio instruments. M'bopo, imperturbable, sat against the wall.

"We won't have to worry much about searchlights," said Williams as the enemy lines drew near, "because it's cloudy enough to conceal us. But a mechanical ear and high-flying scout-sentries could detect us." Into the mouthpiece he barked: "Full speed over the lines at ceiling. If pursued, maneuver to escape. Report immediately if forced to give battle."

Flying over land invisible in the gloom of night, Williams saw coming up the horizon the blue-white glare of searchlights whose beams could probe into the stratosphere itself. Where the beams were absent in long stretches he knew that the uncanny "mechanical ears" were there, and they could detect a single ship miles above. At their terrific speed, the enemy line swung directly below them.

Suddenly a beam swung purposefully in their direction, probed through cloud-mist.

"One of those ears heard us," muttered Williams. "They tried to limelight us."

But after five minutes had passed no swift little scout had zoomed up from the ground, guided by radio, to hang on their tail like an unshakable bulldog, spotting them to chasers. Then it was too late, as the distance between ran into dozens of miles.

Williams' men all reported no pursuit.

"Draw together now on the line between Base Number One and New York," he ordered. "Cabin light on at full. Altitude three miles."

He snapped off the radio and spoke to Terry.

"We'll group with the other ships, Terry. Altitude three miles."

He switched on the cabin lights full and bright. At either wing tip and at the tail of the ovoid cabin, bright crimson lights flashed on. In fifteen minutes, blurs of light triangulated with red points appeared in all directions. At Williams' orders, the ships took up a flying V and stepladder formation, with his ship at the apex.

The ten ships which Williams had picked to accompany him on his mysterious mission were Sansruns, second in speed only to scouts, equipped with two machine-gun nests. Hung in a rack below the cabin were six small drop-bombs. Such ships were used for destroying bases of the enemy or blowing up ammunition dumps, being fast enough to escape all but scouts, and armed enough to have a good chance against combat ships.

At their height, above the commercial lanes, no other ships were sighted as hour after hour they pierced the night, heading into the heart of danger. And Williams alone knew what it was.

They approached New York from the south, having veered from a direct course. Yet they did not turn in the direction of the great metropolis, but skimmed the clouds east of it. As the first faint xanthic glows of dawn appeared, Williams contacted his men and rapidly ran through a series of twice-repeated commands. Then he spoke to Terry and M'bopo.

Looking at the beauty of dawn suffusing the eastern sky, heralding the coming of a late autumn sun, Williams noticed, a half-quadrant away, a spreading fan of shimmering rays of light centered from a spot on the wide bed of ocean. He thought it was an *aurora borealis* until it occurred to him that it was south of the sun.

"What is that mysterious light?" he asked Terry. "It can only be the sun-power experimental station," said the young chemist. "They must have moved it since we last saw it from the stratosphere ship. The giant raft it's set up on is powered to move like any ship."

"But that light! I would say that it's billions of candle-power."

"Billions of heat calories, too!" supplied Terry. "I think I know the reason for it. They produce an enormous amount of sun-power, but having no use for it until it's commercially practicable, I suppose they cast off the excess energy of the day in that way." Williams' eyes widened thoughtfully. A train of thought that started in his mind was abruptly terminated as Terry called: "Here we go—down!"

The planes hummed downward from the misty heights, like phantoms in the ghostly light of dawn. An immense structure loomed up, only partially illuminated as night lights were gradually turned off. Before their altitude lessened by half, New York was visible as a crown of light, and beside it to the east was the lime-whiteness of the Unidum capitol.

"We're discovered already," said Terry, pointing to where a wheeling scout ship with the Unidum emblem on its wings swung in a great circle and sped away toward New York. "They could recognize our ships immediately as part of the rebel forces."

"No matter," said Williams quietly. "Once we land, we're safe for the time being."

Onto the deserted landing roof of the Long Island Tide-station, the tiny fleet landed. Williams told his men to stay with their ships until further orders, then motioned to Terry and M'bopo to follow him.

At the door Joe Manners stood waiting, consternation and bewilderment on his face.

"I got your call during the night," he said. "But for the life of me, I can't figure out—"

"We're here for a little grimmer purpose than that last time," vouchsafed Williams. "Before it was just our lives we were concerned with. Now much more is involved."

"But this whole region is patrolled by Unidum scout ships!" Manners cried nervously. "They'll attack—"

"How can they attack ships on a roof? And they won't dare to try any bombing."

"I see," agreed Manners, calming down. "Strange that the Unidum should leave the tide-station here open to attack."

"They had no suspicion that this might happen," said Williams. "It's always the obvious that escapes notice." He shrugged. "Right now I must know a few things, then perhaps I'll get a workable plan. I came here just to be within striking distance of Molier—who must be put out of the way or stripped of power and authority."

"You mean you came here without authority?" cried Manners. "Oh, I know you are a marshal in the Brotherhood, and a commander in the Air Forces, but surely you are under orders from General Bromberg—"

Williams shook his head. "Strictly on my own, except that Major Agarth sanctioned my leaving with ten ships. I'm a great believer in inspirational effort. When there is trouble I get as near the root of it as possible, worry a couple of plans until they crystallize, then go to it. Spur-of-the-moment things often shape the future. Africa taught me that. Back there at Base One little could be done to forestall the defeat of our forces. It was while talking to Agarth about it that it came to me—no Molier, no tyranny."

"You mean?"

"That my sole aim now is to get Molier!"

"But how, man?" asked Manners, swiftly repeating what Williams had already heard about Molier being unreachable."

"To get Molier," repeated Williams quietly, as though he had not heard. "Assassination, impeachment, overthrow—something!"

"Which is what the Brotherhood has been trying!" There was a note of scorn in Manners' voice for Williams' mad aspirations. "Everything has been tried—everything! By the Brotherhood, the influential heads of industry, *the Unidum itself*! What has happened? No one knows, except that Europe will secede to escape the tangle in America. Molier still plots, while all Unitaria is cracking apart!"

"Hasn't the exposure of Molier and his bunch weakened his power at all? Surely that should cause his impeachment."

"Not yet. His accusers are Bromberg and Hagen, outlaws by Unidum decree. They are rebels, about to be defeated. Molier has convinced Executive Ashley that the Brotherhood is a sheep in wolf's clothing. It's a vicious circle of intrigue. And there's nothing we can do!"

"That, I'm not sure about," declared Williams stoutly. "First, a few questions. This tide-station produces all the electrical current, not only of various cities, but of the capitol. Right?" At a nod from Manners, he went on: "And at the throw of a switch or two, you can cut off that supply?"

"Yes, but—"

"No buts at a time like this. There is no one to prevent such a move, is there?"

"No. The station's employees all work below in the generator and machine rooms. They are not allowed up here. Of course"—he glanced apprehensively into the sky where several striped ships hovered high in the air—"there may be interference from them!"

Williams shrugged. "If they should try any attacking maneuvers, my men will know what to do. And we have all the advantages—stationary aim, massed guns, highly experienced gunners." He turned. "You have a radio with which you can contact the capital?"

"Yes, in the control room."

The cheerful brightness of early morning had now overspread all the region. On the blue blanket of endless ocean, an occasional buff or silvery hyp-marine skimmed the waves. How serene things looked! How peaceful! And yet the affairs of men had reached a crisis. There was a lurking Nemesis that the light of sun and the cheer of day could not dispel like morning mists.

"Now an important question. Have you any food?" Williams smiled. "I can't think properly when I'm hungry."

The well-stocked larders of the tide-station yielded breads and cakes and cold meats. Probably the pantryman was surprised that the superintendent in the sanctum above should suddenly have the appetite of thirty men. But it was not for him to question.

Williams and Terry passed the food to the men. While they were eating, Williams spoke to them.

"Men, we're about as safe right here as we could be anywhere, probably safer than at Base One. Those fellows up there"—he jerked a thumb in the direction of circling Unidum ships—"won't try any bombing, and they can't attack without danger of smashing, to get in machine-gun range. What our next move will be depends on certain things. Until then, stay here with your ships."

As Terry and Williams entered the master control-room where Manners awaited them, a clicking sound was heard.

"The Unidum call-signal!" said Manners, paling. "They'll want to know why rebel ships are here!"

Williams' voice rang clear. "Manners, I'll take the call. You get over to your switchboard and put your hand on the switch that shuts off the current that goes to the capitol."

"What good—"

"Do it!" said Williams quietly, but there was a wealth of command in his tone. "This is the time for initiative and action. What the result will be, I cannot say, but a chance is always worth taking. And as your superior officer in the Brotherhood, I command you both!"

# CHAPTER XVII

Manners hesitated no longer but ran to the control-board where finger-flipped switches could do magic with thousands of kilowatts of electricity.

Williams strode to the wall radio-phone and tripped the loud-speaker lever. An authoritative voice rang through the room.

"Unidum capitol calling Joe Manners, superintendent of the Long Island Tide-station. Eleven ships, apparently part of the rebel forces, are on the landing roof. The Unidum demands an explanation."

"And the Unidum will get an explanation," returned Williams in emphatic tones. "The tide-station is at present in the hands of a marshal of the Brothers of Humanity, in my hands."

"The Unidum accordingly demands that your rebel ships leave at once."

"Leave? Do you think we are playing a game? We are here to stay. If you care to attack, try it. My gunners are experts."

There was a confused murmur from the phone, then another voice spoke, an articulate voice.

"The Unidum is prepared to make an offer, due to the fact that the tide-station is—ah—our special consideration. We offer to waive any charges of treason against you, if you will quietly surrender to the Unidum. We will send over a sealed and signed exemption."

Williams laughed harshly. "You take us for traitors! *No!*"

"Then we shall—"

"You had better listen to me," interrupted Williams. "Unless a demand of mine is granted, Joe Manners, at my command, will cut off the electrical current to the capitol! Your heating equipment will cease to function, your elevators will not run, the ventilating system will not operate, a dozen other little things will paralyze the internal workings of the capitol. Even your radio-phone system will be useless. It also is easy to overload the transformers at the Unidum capitol from this

where reposed several aircraft—warships. But there were only five of the fighting ships.

He turned to the radio-phone: "Ready for battle, men!"

At his instructions, Terry dipped low over the buildings as though to drop a bomb. Uniformed men ran toward the combat ships. They were accepting the challenge!

The Unidum ships arose to where the waiting rebels poised. Eleven to five. Yet it was not to be an unequal skirmish, for the Unidum ships had three guns each, one throwing a small high-powered shell.

The structural conglomeration beneath was sliding away. The people on the sun-power station were simply moving away from the scene of battle, so that falling planes would not smash and ruin expensive apparatus.

Williams spoke into the phone: "Take altitude! No formation! Pick out your antagonist and duel him—*and in the name of heaven, do your best!*"

Terry, startled, saw Williams clambering up the short steel ladder to the trap which opened to the machine-gun nests. Then Terry turned back to his controls grimly. As much depended on his handling of the ship as did on the man above!

At a mile above the water's surface, and well clear of the moving sun-power station came the clash of battle. The rebels depended on their speed and flexibility and greater numbers. But each of the Unidum ships had three grim gunners, so where the real advantage lay could not be said.

To Williams, inexperienced with a machine gun, it seemed like bedlam. There was the ululating roar of speed-shifting motors, the *rat-a-tat* of guns, the flare and sharp report of small shells, the crazy gyration of the plane, the biting cold of rushing air, the helplessness in a strange, open perch. Then, in a flash, it all cleared. There was a gun under his hand, a target now and then.

His finger pulled; his arm vibrated; his hand guided the handle, pointing the muzzle at a striped ship that swung downward past them. He shouted aloud when one of the gunners slumped into his cockpit. First blood! A flash from the big gun, and something shrieked past his ear.

*Sarto*! That was close! But he must keep his eyes everywhere and swing the gun without hesitation. And so it went on for what seemed hours, but in reality were minutes.

Williams' men fought their best, and it was just a little better than the best of the Unidum airmen. Ship after ship spun out of control and fluttered to the ocean, or caught fire to fall like a meteor. Then only two ships remained, both rebels.

Williams descended to the cabin.

"We've won, Terry. But at—a price." He shook his head and called the other ship: "Descend and follow. We take over the sun-power station immediately."

The reply from the other ship was delayed, then a voice, pain-filled: "Yes, Commander—we descend—gunner killed—wounded. Good-by and—good luck."

The other ship, behaving erratically, bespoke the weakening hand of a dying pilot.

"But you've not died in vain," said Williams softly. "*I swear it*!"

The other ship lurched drunkenly, then plunged downward.

"Well, Terry, it's up to us." Williams' voice was husky. "Where's M'bopo?"

"Why, he followed you out! Didn't he—"

"Lord! Then he must have fallen. I didn't see him."

Already numbed by the many deaths during the past hour, the loss of the Bantu seemed the final strain.

But Williams breathed deeply and fastened his attention on the sun-power station as Terry landed the ship on it. The two stepped out with pistols in hand, menacing the small crowd that had gathered, before Williams spoke to the half-dozen men in the blue capes of Scientists.

"This sun-power station is now in the hands of the Brotherhood, or the rebels, as you choose to call us. With your armed escort gone, you have no choice but to recognize my authority."

"We realize that," said one of the Scientists, "and we're glad of it!"

"Glad to be in rebel hands?" asked Williams incredulously.

"Certainly. We would never have let those five Unidum ships attack you had we been able to prevent it. Let me… Will you please order that man away from the gun? He looks ready to open fire any minute!"

Williams whirled—and cried with joy. In the second of the gun cockpits, was M'bopo. With his hands on the gun, he looked indeed ready to spout flame and lead.

"Come down from there!" shouted Williams in Bantu dialect.

The black man clambered from the gun cupola and leaped to the landing floor. Williams strode back to the impatient Scientists.

"Now, sirs, if you will explain—"

"Just this," said the previous spokesman. "We, aboard this experimental sun-power station, of course, have been in touch with national events via radio, and have from the first favored the Brotherhood. We realize the insidiousness of Brain-control and the threat of brain-enslavement. Practically all our lives we six here have labored to produce power from the sun, and our goal is near. Despairing indeed was the news that Molier was making a bid for absolute dictatorship. When the Brotherhood announced its opposition, and military revolution broke out, we hoped Molier would be broken. Apparently"—his voice became heavy—"it can't be done."

"And perhaps it can!" contradicted Williams. "With your help, with your pledges to give me any and all aid, the tide may be turned yet!"

"I give that pledge myself," said the Scientist. Others nodded vigorously.

"Would you even"—Williams swept an eye at the jungle of towered apparatus surrounding them—"willingly endanger all this, your life work?"

The Scientist swallowed but answered quickly.

"We of the sun-power station have more than once wished we could save Unitaria from threatened evil, at any price. But in what way can science serve?"

"How soon can you reach New York with this motored raft?" Williams asked.

"Possibly by dawn tomorrow."

"Can you swing those night beams which throw off excess sun-energy in any direction?"

The Scientist pursed his lips thoughtfully. "Yes, with a little alteration in machinery."

"Good!" cried Williams exultantly. "Now, have you an all-wave transmitter?"

"In the building there," said the Scientist.

"I must get in touch with General Bromberg!" shouted Williams as he madly dashed to the building.

A man seated before the control panel of an allwave radio looked up inquiringly.

"Eighteen point two centimeters—full power, and hurry!" barked Williams. "Ask for General Bromberg!"

# CHAPTER XVIII

Quietly Terry stepped into the room, just in time to begin coding a message Williams wrote hastily. The Brotherhood's code had never been cracked by the Unidum intelligence service. The vowels of its key word were changed every ten hours by the clock. Agarth answered from Base One. "Who calls?"

"Williams—Marshal Williams."

"Great guns! I had no hope of hearing your voice again. General Bromberg is ill, Williams."

"Then listen, Agarth! Take this code. I'll give it twice."

The message translated was:

> YOU MUST HOLD OUT AT BASE ONE UNTIL DAWN TOMORROW. FIGHT AS YOU'VE NEVER FOUGHT BEFORE, BUT HOLD OUT! THE SUN-POWER STATION, THE MOST POWERFUL AND INVINCIBLE WAR-MACHINE IN THE WORLD, IS IN MY HANDS. AT DAWN TOMORROW
> I WILL THREATEN TO BURN THE CAPITOL TO A CINDER IF MOLIER IS NOT OUSTED.

In code came back:

> WILL HOLD OUT IF HADES FALLS!

The gray of dawn revealed a huge bulk in the East River before the capitol of Unitaria. Like a sentient giant the sun-power station frowned majestically over the seat of government. Buzzing aircraft hovered like flies, darting and spinning in curiosity. Suddenly a blinding beam of light shot upward from the internal mazes of the station, and two unlucky ships whiffed into flame. The beam swung awesomely downward until it just barely touched the peak of a dome on a capitol building. The peak glowed red, then white, then fell away molten.

What internal revolution had occurred in the capitol after Williams' ultimatum the watchers aboard the sun-power station did not know. That the Unidum had fallen away from Molier, they did know, and also knew that the Unidum was prepared to call off hostilities against the Brotherhood, and negotiate. The sun-power Scientists were in hearty agreement.

Two hours after dawn, a ship arose from a roof landing of the capitol, engines beating frantically. From somewhere came the flash and report of an anti-aircraft gun. A part of the rising ship's wing crumpled, and for seconds the craft gyrated madly downward. Then the pilot must have regained partial control for, sagging in the air, about to plunge downward, it miraculously kept an even keel and coasted to land in the center of the man-made island of sun-mirrors.

From the badly smashed cabin crawled a tall, gaunt figure. His clothing indicated that he was one of the two executive heads of Unitaria. His blue cape marked him as a Scientist. He straightened up to face a group of men who instantly recognized him.

Standing at the head of the group, facing him, was a robust man whose tanned face indicated that he had known rigorous climates. The gaunt man, wild-eyed, poured out a flood of words. The tanned man answered sternly. The gaunt one again broke out in a torrent of language, and the other man made a threatening move toward him.

Of a sudden the gaunt man's hand whipped into his robe and came out with a tiny tubular object. It was pointed straight at the tanned man and from it came a dull blue flash. But the charge of the lightning pistol did not find its mark; a man had leaped between the two. It was M'bopo who sagged to the wooden landing.

For a moment everyone froze. Then, with a shout, the tanned man leaped for his gaunt antagonist in quivering rage. The gaunt man seemed to have the strength of a madman, so that even the other's steel muscles were matched. Suddenly the blue flash again appeared. The gaunt man fell.

The tanned man looked at his vanquished foe a moment, then turned to kneel beside his Bantu comrade, reverently.

Molier, arch-tyrant of 1973, was dead.

Earl Hackworth could hardly control his voice.

"Tell me all about it, Dan—Terry. How did you get away from the tide-station? How did you meet Agarth? How—"

"All in good time, Earl," said Williams. "The thing now is—Lila!"

"Oh, yes, yes," agreed Hackworth. The excitement of seeing them after weeks of separation—and eternities of events—had thrown him into a turmoil. "She's still in the hospital, sleeping as peacefully as ever."

"What a relief!" breathed Terry, and added softly: "Lila!"

Then he glanced at Williams. "But—Agarth called—don't you remember? He will be here, and with some sort of parade in your honor with him, to take you to witness the ceremonies which take the Brain-control Act and the Eugenics Law from the statutes, and the formal announcement of Europe's agreement to veto secession."

"Terry," answered Williams slowly, "you've been with me through thick and thin. You've stuck with me even when you must have thought I'd gone mad. I'm going to the hospital with you now."

"But Agarth—"

"Hang Agarth—for the time being! Come on!" During the drive, no word was spoken. Terry, face aglow, seemed lost in dreams. Williams seemed depressed. He could not forget M'bopo, who was to be buried in state.

At the Unidum Hospital Hackworth said to the attendant: "Miss Lila Hackworth, Room Two-o-two-four."

"I'm sorry, sir," said the white-clad woman, "but she's gone!"

"*Gone*?"

The word seemed to echo and re-echo in thunder. Terry was shouting it incredulously. Williams placed a hand on his shoulder.

"You must be mistaken," Hackworth said confidently. "I saw her just yesterday. She's that sleeping case."

"I know, sir. But she *is* gone!"

"What do you mean!" cried Terry.

"Oh, I knew I shouldn't have let him—" The woman seemed about to become hysterical. "But what else could I do? Professor Jorgen—he's superintendent of Unidum hospitals and has authority—he took her away last night."

"Last night he had not a shred of authority!" shouted Terry. "He's to be exiled!"

"Well, he had a pistol in his hand, and the look in his eyes—horrible!" The woman lowered her voice. "We didn't dare try to stop him."

"But why should he take Lila away?" asked Hackworth tremulously.

"In mental disorder," said Williams, "sometimes an idea grows to mountainous proportions. Perhaps the exasperation of being balked in marrying Lila has obsessed him. Where did he take her?"

"I don't know, sir. But he has a private summer home at Edgewood, in the Catskill Mountains. And his plane went north."

"Let's go," said Williams grimly.

A half-hour later, Hackworth piloted his Sansrun away from New York to the north. Terry sat pale and drawn.

"Hurry, Hackworth!" he pleaded, agonized. "That madman might kill her!"

"Not that," soothed Williams. "He probably took her to his home, tried to waken her but being unsuccessful, likely by now some other fancy will be occupying him."

Not a mile east of Edgewood, in a quiet setting of hills and forest, they found Jorgen's woodland retreat. As Hackworth brought his ship down they saw another ship there that could only be Jorgen's.

Williams held up a hand and whispered: "Let's reconnoiter. Hearing us land, he may be laying for us with a gun."

The low, rambling cottage had many windows and at each of them Williams, with a lightning pistol in his hand, looked in stealthily. He saw nothing. When they had completely circled the house Williams looked puzzled.

"Looks deserted, as though it's been shut up since the summer. Could it be he isn't here, after all?"

"But his ship!" whispered Hackworth. "He must be here!"

Williams thought a moment.

"We'll try the door."

It opened squeakily to reveal a dusty hallway.

"Tracks in the dust!" said Terry.

Williams nodded and followed them. They led to the open door of a lighted room. An unmistakable odor came to them—a chemical laboratory! Williams raced into the room, with Terry not a step behind.

"I've been waiting for you," said a calm voice. "No, don't shoot. I have this needle above the girl's heart!"

Professor Jorgen, heavy-browed and thin-lipped, stood over the limp form of Lila on a couch. In his hand a large hypodermic was poised. A downward thrust would pierce her heart.

In utter silence the three glared. Jorgen's lips were half snarling, half smiling.

"I heard your plane land and surmised someone had come for the girl. This girl would be my wife, but for a strange malady. She's mine, do you hear?"

"Just a minute, Professor Jorgen," said Williams. "Perhaps—"

"Nothing you can say will interest me. Listen to what *I* have to say!" The eyes gleamed with devils. "A strange malady has put this girl into a trance, as though a witch had cast an evil spell upon her. But it is no sorcery. Science can cure her. I am a Scientist!" His voice had a remnant of former pride in it. "Since last night I have been working, knowing I must awaken her before she dies of under-nourishment. In this hypodermic is a fluid that will awaken her. You can't stop me, either! And when she awakes, I will marry her, because she loves me!"

Williams felt Terry straining forward, and breathed a word in his ear.

"Wait!"

He looked back at Jorgen. "Professor Jorgen," said Williams quickly. "You mistake us. We haven't come for the girl."

"What?" barked the Scientist.

"We care nothing about the girl. We are here in behalf of the Unidum. Due to your past services, you are to be given your freedom."

For a moment eyes bored at Williams with uncanny cunning. Williams watched like a hawk. That hand…

"Not exiled," Jorgen muttered. "Free! They won't prosecute me!"

Seconds stretched into a dozen eternities, while he blinked, alternately suspicious and incredulous, perplexed. Then his hand which had poised so long over the girl's heart, drew slowly upward. Williams watched as inch by inch it was raised, as the Scientist gradually gave credence to the statement.

The moment had come. A dull blue flash leaped from Williams' upraised pistol. Terry yelled and dashed forward, for with tigerlike quickness, the man had plunged the needle straight for Lila's heart.

Terry slumped beside the couch and broke into dry sobs. "Lila! Darling! Am I too late to call you back to life?"

Her pallid face looked like the face of death, and the heartbroken Terry bowed his head in numbing sorrow. He did not see the two men behind him whisper excitedly, nor did he see the fluttering of the girl's eyelids. Dulled with the mists of long sleep, the soft brown eyes opened, fastened on the face beside her, and cleared suddenly.

"Terry!"

A moment later Terry descended from the clouds enough to wonder about that death-stroke that he had apparently seen pierce the girl's heart. Hackworth pointed to Lila's breast. The hypodermic, driven downward by a hand suddenly bereft of life, had merely tangled in her heavy hospital gown without scratching the girl's skin.

Williams, with tears of happiness in his eyes, turned to his cousin as the young couple clung to each other.

"Earl," Williams said, "we can wait outside. I really feel quite unnecessary in here. Don't you?"

www.ingramcontent.com/pod-product-compliance
Lightning Source LLC
Chambersburg PA
CBHW020657180626
46816CB00003B/1326